NORTH BY NORTHEAST
AND OTHER STORIES

NORTH BY NORTHEAST AND OTHER STORIES

P.S. Thangkhiew

PARTRIDGE
A Penguin Random House Company

To order additional copies of this book, contact
Partridge India
000 800 10062 62
orders.india@partridgepublishing.com

www.partridgepublishing.com/india

THE BIG MATCH

It was a glorious April morning in Shillong town. There was no sign to indicate that this was the month which normally heralded the onset of the annual monsoon. There was not a hint of cloud in the overarching deep blue sky, a type of blue found only in those hill stations and small towns, which have been bypassed by the smokestacks of an emerging economy. A gentle breeze played around the ground and caressed the marigolds preening in the sun. The cherry blossom trees lining the left side at the beginning of the first fairway were still in bloom. A pair of songbirds perched on one of the trees added their chorus to this scene of perfect harmony. The ninety year old clubhouse with its imposing green roof, chimney stack and French windows was situated on the top of the knoll and with the lush and expansive 18th green in the foreground looked like a scene from a picture postcard. A literary minded onlooker would have quoted Shakespeare's 'April hath put a spirit of youth in everything'.

The golfer, whose name was Don Lang—lining up his second shot on the 18th fairway was seemingly oblivious to these sylvan surroundings. Lang in fact had done his Masters in English Literature from Delhi University and the opening lines; 'April is the cruelest month . . .' from T.S. Eliot's 'Wasteland' were resonating in his mind. He took a deep breath and closed his eyes as if to shut out reality. The immediate reason for his present state of mind was not far to see. His golf ball lay at the foot of one of the century old pine trees dividing the 1st and 18th fairways. The ball had landed in the worst possible place for anyone planning on hitting a regulation shot on to the green. This was the crux of the situation.

Lang needed to land his ball on the 18th green to have even a ghost of a chance of winning the game. And win the game he must! Yet to land the ball on the green from this location on the fairway was perhaps a one in a million chance. The normal line of the ball was obstructed by a row of trees and the only option was to hook the ball at ludicrous angle of almost 120 degrees. Bubba Watson had achieved this seemingly impossible shot when he won the Masters Tournament at Augusta in 2012 in a sudden death play-off on the second hole against the South African, Louis Oosthuizen.

But Lang was painfully aware that he was no Bubba Watson; and he was not a left hander. He was slightly above average height and he was not even physically in prime shape. Despite a constant attempt to shed his extra pounds, his paunch was still noticeable. And, he was only a capable amateur player with a dodgy nine handicap though competent enough to compete in the various Pro-Am tournaments being staged in different parts of the country. 'Damn it'! He uttered, if he did not manage to land his second shot on the 18th green, the consequences would be disastrous to say the least. Losing was a situation, which could not even be remotely contemplated. For this outcome would lead to an upheaval of his entire life and the irrevocable loss of everything he held dear.

Till the other day Don Lang was the envy of his friends and colleagues, happy, well off and with a loving family. Now, how did he get into this situation where even suicide was being contemplated? Perhaps because of his present dilemma, his mind wandered to the 'flashbacks' of those incidents which had led to his present stressful situation . . . the weekly four-ball golf game about five years earlier where the normal wager till that point in time was a bottle of beer or two for the victors. He remembered that fateful morning teaming up with one of his bureaucrat friends against two other players who were businessmen and who had suggested that they could compete for a small wager. Rather than turning down the suggestion and thereby losing face, the two bureaucrats had acquiesced. In this routine but significant contest, he and his partner had ended up winning a small sum of a thousand rupees. He recalled the time when he began to avoid office work so that he could 'shoot the shaft' again and again . . . and then when he got bitten by the bug.

Over successive months, the stakes had steadily increased and the betting became an addiction. He would even play three full rounds daily. Office work was now totally neglected and within no time at all he lost his job as a senior vice president in one of those many private sector firms, which had sprung up riding on the boom of the information technology revolution. In fact, he had left his job at IMC, a government corporation lured by the pay packet and perks of a position in the private sector. And again that was another mistake. His wife had warned him that leaving his secure job, albeit poorly paid, for a high paying private sector job was not worth the risk in the long term. Now he was without a job, covering up his disappearances in the mornings and not telling his wife about his current state of affairs.

. . . Yes, till the other day, Lang was still not in the doldrums and financially was still relatively comfortable. He had further improved his game with all the regular practice and was ahead in the winnings. Betting between amateur players in a golf game is popular pastime and many a small fortune has been won or lost on a golf course. The Shillong Golf Club was no exception and attracted golfers from all over the country. With no shortage of competitors, he was playing on a regular basis and was being able to put meals on the table without much difficulty. But one can never predict the outcome of a match especially in the context of the well-documented uncertainties of the game of golf. And yes, come to think of it, lately he had been not doing too well. Lady Luck, such an important ingredient in any game had briefly deserted him. The rub of the green was not favoring him. Putts were not going in and missing by even one-tenth of an inch. These yips were becoming significant and he was not being able to identify his shortcomings. Even so, he could still keep his head above the water. The final straw though was the losses he incurred in gambling with fellow members. What started off as a time-pass in the card room of the Golf Club soon became an obsession and in no time at all, he was being hounded by I.O.Us brandished by all his creditors. His other losses incurred in gambling and betting on the popular betting game of 'teer' was another contributing factor to his present pecuniary condition. He could not possibly hide forever from his wife the fact that he had lost his job.

He knew he was lucky in his marriage. No doubt, it was rocky in the initial years due to the differences in their background and upbringing. His detractors including some members of his wife's family had sniped behind his back that the marriage was doomed from the beginning and it would not last for even a year. But over the 18 odd years, they had developed a relationship based on trust and communication. And despite the differences which sometimes threatened their relationship, they never broke preset rules, such as never raking up issues concerning their different religious beliefs and never arguing in front of their children. He realized that he was lucky to find a partner who did not nag and was not subject to mood swings which could upset the environment in the household. Despite the occasional arguments which are common in all relationships, communication between them never broke down. Now in his late forties, the light which lit up their relationship in their courtship days was still to fade and rather, it had become more enveloping and subtle.

And he also acknowledged her thrift and practicality enabling them to move to a three bedroom house in a leafy suburb of the city. Furthermore, she brought up their two daughters without intruding too much on his golf time and totally committed herself to the care and needs of the family. Her cooking skills were unparalleled to the extent that friends and family literally queued up for invitations as every meal was a unique feeding experience in itself.

Therefore, to save his marriage and all the things he held dear, Don Lang devised a 'plan'. The objective of the plan was to win 'big' and with the winnings, he would park some funds in a fixed deposit scheme and safely invest the rest in mutual funds and government securities. The first part of his 'plan' centered on him setting up of 'a one to one' golf game played on a match-play format with very high stakes and emerging as the winner was naturally a part of his 'plan'. The second part of the plan would entail Lang giving up this golf betting and gambling once and for all. He would again try to get his old job back. Even if he failed to find employment, he could still live off the interest and maybe with some good return on his investments could even go for a holiday overseas with the family— perhaps to Phuket? And wouldn't his wife be happy? For she loved seeing places and traveling. And there had been less and less of travelling since the time he lost his regular job . . .

Nevertheless, there was one hitch. Lang did not have the money upfront to deposit the stakes for the match. And Rs. 100 lakhs was the amount which had been agreed upon. It was also agreed that each player had to deposit the cash in the nearby bank branch of the State Bank of India located opposite the now defunct Race Course, in an escrow account opened in the name of the Club Secretary. This official was disliked by Don Lang for his bossy behavior and for flouting his authority particularly with the newer members. Though Lang did not want to have any dealings with him, he had no choice and in any case, this issue was minor in the overall scheme of things.

Lang realized that he needed to obtain the money somehow or the other. No one was loaning him any big sums of money even those he considered as close friends. No one was willing to even stand as his guarantor. They knew about his present financial condition and besides he no longer had the security guaranteed by a regular job. He considered approaching his cousin, Arvan, who was a senior bureaucrat and whose word could open many doors. But he did not want to either being admonished or take the risk of letting his cousin down. The only option left was therefore to mortgage his house, place his car and his wife's jewelry, as security for obtaining a loan from the local mafia. Despite the risks involved, he was cocksure that he would emerge triumphant in the 'big match'.

The day for the big match quickly arrived. The Rs 100 lakh prize and his future were now in his own hands. Don Lang realized that he was now literally 'the master of his fate and the captain of his soul'. Three set of games had been arranged between local players and those golfers who had come from outside Shillong. Stakes for the other two were comparatively nominal. The contests were arranged so that the contestants played in the same four ball group. In all there were about a hundred contestants vying to win the prestigious Shillong Open. Except for a chosen few, no one was aware of the high stakes game being played between two players. However, word had got around that Lang was involved in a high stake contests and there were quite a number of spectators who had come to witness the excitement. It was also whispered that some of the wealthier businessmen had placed bets on the outcome of his contest.

Waiting for his turn to tee off on the first hole, (his group was third as per the draw), Don Lang tried his best to maintain his composure. He kept his mind focused entirely on the contest at hand. As he was warming up he was told that his opponent was some stockbroker from Kolkata with a 7 handicap. He was confident that this person could not be able match the advantage Lang enjoyed playing on his home course. He was all but sure that that his opponent had not played in the challenging and difficult Shillong Golf Course before or he would have known about it. Of course he would have been a regular player in the Tollygunge Golf Course in Calcutta and other similar courses in Jamshedpur and Digboi. But they were courses with flat fairways and where the technique of swinging the club was almost always the same. In the Shillong Golf Course, most of the fairways were undulating or sloped steeply and for the uninitiated, every second or third shot presented a challenge even for those players used to playing on undulating courses.

It was now Lang's turn to tee off. He felt relaxed and comfortable. His front nine (first nine holes that is) went off like a dream. He was completely focused all the while remembering at the right time all the training and tips learnt from YouTube golf swing tutorial videos. More importantly his muscle memory was not letting him down. He claimed the first five holes, and shared the next four. With a lead of four going into the back nine (last nine holes), he was confident of maintaining a lead till the culmination of the match. Then, his nightmare began on the 10th hole. A combination of overconfidence followed by an attack of nerves made him lose his focus for one crucial moment. He muffed his second shot and the ball shanked off his 5 iron and went out of bounds. Lang had to again repeat the shot. He now needed to clear the hazard in front of the green with his reshot to muster a bogey, i.e. complete the hole with a one over par. The green lay straight ahead at a distance of about 225 yards. He knew that making the shot was quite possible as he had done it before only about a month or so ago. Brimming with confidence and a quiet determination, Lang took out the Callaway 3 wood, presented by his old school friend settled in New York and who was doing extremely well as a software engineer. This was his favorite club because of this association.

Taking a deep breath and relaxing his muscles Don Lang swung through the ball. The swing was picture perfect and one that even Tiger Woods would have admired. The ball was a soft feel Newing brand, made in Japan and had a triple core design which was so innovative that it had yet to be approved by the USGA. He could feel the impact between club head and ball was at the sweetest spot and the projectile sailed into the air zooming to its pre-determined destination. Yes, he thought! He could certainly halve the hole as his opponent was trying to make a par from about 10 feet. But suddenly . . . at the point where the ball was coming close to the end of its natural trajectory, and about to touch down on the green perhaps no further than 1 feet from the pin, a gust of wind originating from a 'north by northeast' direction unexpectedly interrupted the flight of his ball. To his horror, the ball lost some of its velocity and though it landed on the rough of the green, rolled backwards into the water hazard. He dropped another stroke and lost the hole. This reversal badly jangled his nerves and dented his confidence.

A sense of impending dread overpowered Lang's entire being as he stood on the 11th tee box next to the breakfast hut. Even the soothing voice of his old caddy did not have any effect. It was almost all downhill after this reversal. He hit bad shots on the 11th, 12th and 13th holes which were considered amongst the easiest on the course. His once comfortable lead had quickly evaporated and he was now trailing his opponent by the 15th hole. However, he recovered his composure on the next two holes and with some audacious shot making he could manage to even the contest on the 17th hole and thus become 'all square'. Now, the results of the last hole would decide the winner and literally decide the future course of his life. Now he could understand what 'on the bubble' meant!

The 18th hole at the Shillong Golf Course will not win any recognition for its length. It is a par 4 and only about 415 yards long. However, it is an intimidating hole. Firstly, its driveway is narrow, slopes steeply to the right and bounded on the left by a public road linking the Golf Links market place and the Police Training Centre and carrying on to Mawpat Village. Balls landing on this road are out of bounds. Once a player commits this error, he invariably loses the hole. On the right of the above fairway was the 1st fairway and though not out of bounds, there was a line of old pine trees which divided these two fairways. A ball landing at the foot of these mute sentinels spells trouble for the player as they obscure his sight of the green and obstruct the line of the ball.

For the second time in his life, Don Lang, a self professed atheist prayed to his Creator. He remembered praying hard when he was flying from Gauhati to Delhi and the jet encountered extreme turbulence in mid flight. This time round, it was a desperate prayer to the Almighty to ensure that his opponent should spoil or muff his 'tee shot'. He could barely watch as his tormentor placed his ball on the tee and launched into his shot. Yes! Lang's prayers were indeed answered. The drive was not perfect in length and line as it dangerously skirted the road line on the left and seemed to be landing in the hazard along the fairway. But, 'oh bloody hell'!; it seemed that God was deaf to his pleas as his opponent's ball landed on a friendly contour and rolled onto a spot near the 150-yard stone marker. This was an area from where the second shot would be child's play. He knew that anybody could play the shot with an 8 iron and the worst result his opponent could possibly achieve would be a par, i.e. finish the hole in 4 strokes or even a birdie at best. Lang who was a self professed atheist till the other day, internally raved and ranted at all those gods who were so impervious to his entreaties. He could not rely on divine intervention anymore. His drive had to better that of his opponent's. It simply had to . . . He took out his Callaway Razr 9.5 loft driver and addressed the ball. All his concentration was now focused on the shot at hand. He aural senses did not even register the protesting sounds emanating from an engine of an overloaded truck toiling up the hill to Mawpat Village. All the sympathizers and those bettors who had placed their bets on him were watching and silently willing him to win. He addressed the ball and yes! Wonder of wonders! It was a sublime shot straight out of a YouTube training video.

Alas was it "to be or not to be . . . ?" The ball did literally bisect the fairway in two but bounced off an unforgiving slope on the fairway and rolled slowly down onto the right. It paused briefly as if to ponder its route.

Don Lang watched the flight of his ball with bated breath and willed it to stop but it continued to trickle down and eventually nestled behind the foot of one of the thickest pine trees . . . there was a collective groan from the onlookers.

Don Lang stood over the ball and tried to figure out a way on how to negotiate his second shot round the cruel branches and the unyielding twigs. Even his considerable experience and his knowledge of shot making could not assist him in any decision on club and shot selection. Though he had watched Bubba Watson's seemingly impossible shot on TV, when he clinched the Masters, he was not conversant with the technique. He vaguely knew that the ball at the time of address had to be aligned with the right foot and the club face closed to the extent possible. His opponent stood nearby wearing an expression which was part gloating and part anticipation. Lang had a strong urge to knock in his skull with a golf club. He controlled himself and shook his head to clear out all such murderous thoughts. He took out his 8 iron club and addressed the ball. He could hear the whistling sound inside his head which was a sign that his blood pressure was dangerously high. Tension, as every golfer was aware is the enemy of a golf swing and his body was all tight and taut. He visualized the shot, took a deep breath, closed his mind to all sight and sound and with his head down swung his club at the ball . . .

Oh shit! Lang knew even before the club made contact that he had lost it. His backswing was jerky and caused his hip to rotate ahead of the club in the middle of its descent. He groaned in despair and with the contest surely lost, he was now certain that his comfortable life was now surely over . . . his future now terribly bleak. His wife would surely throw him out and make him shift to his mother's house. If only he had reined in his arrogance well in time? Now, without the shadow of a doubt, his arrogance and his obsession would have serious negative consequences?

Lang watched with bated breath as his ball sliced to the right narrowly missing a pine branch. He could barely look as it sailed over the steep slope and its place of landing would have surely been the rooftop of the house belonging to the shifty headman of the locality across the road. But Lady Luck intervened in his favor. A gust of wind travelling in a north by northeasterly direction and perhaps heralding the onset of the first monsoon rains significantly altered the flight and direction of the ball. It struck the uppermost part of a eucalyptus tree, the only survivor of a long forgotten World Environment Day tree plantation program. The ball deviated again to the left and 'miraculously' landed on the 18th green, a mere 6 inches from the hole. His birdie putt was now a mere formality. His opponent could only manage a par. Victory for Don Lang! There was a loud applause from the onlookers. The prize he sought was won! His big match was finally over and was his new lease of life about to begin?

SLINGS AND ARROWS

I was not meant to be doing this. Considering my upbringing and family background, I was not meant to be a 'hitwoman', an assassin?! I was meant to be a self-assured and well paid consultant in a company like Price Waterhouse Coopers. And here I was, uncomfortably perched going on five hours on a trunk of a magnificent pine tree in the thick forest situated adjacent to the 8th hole of the Shillong Golf Course. It was getting chilly despite my North Face anorak, as the sun eased itself slowly down west of the Shillong Peak. The shadows cast by the tall trees on the grounds slowly lengthened and seemed to come vividly to life as the sun descended. The rolling lush fairways of the 8th and 9th holes with this magnificent sunset as a backdrop gloriously showcased Mother Nature in all its grandeur. The little brook bordering the adjoining 9th fairway babbled along its confused path, with the wild golden yellow marigolds nodding their heads in the pine scented breeze as if keeping time with the murmurings of the silvery water. The manicured fairways further enhanced this image of serene beauty. Here and there cymbidiums lit up the forests with their splashes of pink and white colors. But this sylvan harmony was only external and did not calm the dark storms in my mind.

Till the other day, we were a happy and contented family. There were four of us, my parents, my sister

Ophelia, and me. My father whose name was Don Lang was an affable soul and being a student of English Literature was an admirer of Shakespeare. He named me after Rosalind, the heroine of 'As You Like it". I was quite independent thinking and confident like the character I was named after. We lived in our own house, with our own bedrooms and a big garden. We never lacked for anything and were well looked after by a loyal pair of servants. I studied in the elite Pinewood School and excelled not only in my studies but also in extracurricular activities. The school had produced a good number of students who excelled in sharpshooting and who had gone on to win medals in national and international competitions. My instructors were of the opinion that I had outstanding potential and predicted that with the proper training and discipline would pick up even an Olympic medal. I managed to combine my hobby and studies successfully and graduated at the head of my class in the Class 12 Board exams. I then applied for admission into the Indian Institutes of Technology and after 6 months of intensive studying, cracked the entrance exam and joined the B (Tech) course in Electronics, at IIT, Delhi. Though I had to give up my hobby of gun shooting, the future never looked brighter. I held my own amongst the best of the best students of the country.

The midnight phone call from my sister hysterically calling me back saying Dad was very ill; the frantic last minute boarding of a flight to Gauhati was permanently scarred in my memory . . . When I arrived in Shillong; it was the beginning of a hellish nightmare. Dad had apparently committed suicide in Ward's Lake unable to cope with his misfortunes. He had suffered heavy losses in playing high stakes in golf games, of all things! It transpired that he had lost his job 4 years earlier due to his obsession with the game and borrowing heavily to cover his losses. In desperation, he had pawned all of Mom's jewelry (except her wedding ring and her gold chain since she wore them at all times), and even mortgaged our house to pay off his creditors He had then staked all he had and Mom's (without her knowledge, of course) and lost everything in a winner take all round played in the Shillong Golf Course. Over the next few days, I was told that he once won 'big' (Rupees 1 crore) which would have enabled him to permanently put 'dinner on the table' but it seemed that his addiction got the better of him in the end.

I never liked the game of golf because it required patience and constant practice much to Dad's disappointment. However, with my shooting skills I would often accompany him in winter on bird shoots to jungles and forests in the rural areas, and other places and bring home plenty of elusive jungle fowl, Khaleej pheasants and the big turtle neck pigeons. The semi-automatic .22 Remington Viper rifle was my favorite weapon then. I recall shooting three snipes in quick succession in a paddy field near Marngar Village much to the amazement of my father and other hunting companions. The snipe in general can only be shot with a shotgun using Number 8 shells due to their explosive speed and elusiveness.

Our creditors drove us out of hearth and home. We were forced to depend on the kindness of our relatives whose numbers rapidly dwindled as the months went by. We had to endure constant condescension and the false sympathy of our hosts. Finally, we ended up staying in a rented house on the poorer sections of the town living a hand to mouth existence. This locality in an area called Fourth Furlong was the refuge for economic migrants from other parts of India and from Nepal and Bangladesh. It teemed with undesirable characters and murders and assaults were very common. Municipal services were non-existent and we had to collect water from a community tap, standing in line under a hot sun for long hours. Electrical supply was intermittent at best and the stench from open drains and garbage permeated the air. Fourth Furlong boasted of the highest crime rate in the city and we were lucky that we were not badly affected in any way.

Remunerative work was difficult to find especially in a contractor driven economy. We did not have the political contacts needed for getting any government appointment. Yes, from being upper middle class folks being chauffeured around, we were now barely surviving on Dad's meager pension, which Mom was trying to supplement by knitting and doing needlework for a local boutique. After struggling to make ends meet for quite a long time, a ship of hope appeared over the horizon. Ophelia had appeared in an exam for recruiting candidates for the prestigious State Civil Service. She successfully cleared the written exam and only an interview now stood between her and a secure future. I was hopeful that I would even be able to resume my interrupted studies and get on with my life; or so I thought!

One evening when reaching home, after finishing my duties as a salesgirl in the local KFC, my mother sadly informed that a week earlier, she had pawned her remaining jewelry and with her little savings 'presented' the entire amount to a member of the State Public Service Commission to guarantee my sister's appointment. But when the results were declared earlier in the day, my sister's name did not figure on the list. Frantic efforts to contact the 'friendly member' and at the very least recover some portion of the 'investment' proved futile. Even my father' cousin, Arvan who was a senior bureaucrat could not intervene in the matter. Almost all the members of the Commission enjoyed political patronage due to mutual back scratching and punishment for acts of wrongdoing were unheard of. We found out later that the member had gone abroad on an 'official' holiday.

Mom never recovered from this misfortune and passed away within a year. Ophelia and I moved in with my mother's younger sister in Mawpat Village who like Mrs. Mann in "Oliver Twist' was more interested in extracting every ounce of energy from us rather than contribute to our well being. Our daily existence revolved around back breaking chores with insults and scolding being a daily background chorus. In front of my eyes, Ophelia slowly wasted away and literally died in my arms.

Without even a bachelor's degree, my future looked bleak indeed. Suicide was a constant companion in my mind. The Nirvana song 'Come as you are' was a constant refrain. Over the months, my resentment against the ruling elite became a deep hatred for the 'system', the government and all those members of society who it seemed were prospering because of their decadence and corruption and exploitation of the less advantaged sections of society.

Eventually, I joined one of those insurgent outfits that espoused the cause of winning independence for fulfilling the race's destiny but were only motivated by self aggrandizement and making easy money. Because of my anger with the system I became committed to any movement that advocated violent means to end the rule of the ruling elite. After being properly indoctrinated, I was deputed for 'training' to a neighboring country. With my shooting skills, and under the tutelage of battle hardened trainers, I became an expert sniper. I remembered my first 'kill'; a corrupt politician who bled to death on a parking lot in the city center. I felt no remorse whatsoever.

My number of 'kills' increased and the reward for my capture or information about my whereabouts also increased, I could not trust anyone and I became a loner. I had to adopt many disguises, both male and female and was always on the move. All the values and morals learnt and absorbed during my formative years were rapidly being nullified and rubbed out by the number of kills I had achieved. Organized religion with all its dogma and the pretentious attitude of pastors and priests was something I abhorred. In those times of loneliness and schizophrenia, I came to realize that the only remaining buffer between me and insanity were some of those Shakespearean plays made familiar to me by an English literature teacher of the local college where I studied. I liked the four tragic plays and the ability of the heroes to cope with adversity and death. I equally liked the great comedies. The themes, motifs and symbolism and the thread of humanism permeating the writings of The Bard, his dissection of the follies of human life and his celebration of the nobility of the common man were made alive and relevant for the modern times by this gifted teacher. 'As You Like It' in particular was one of my favorites. In retrospect, my appreciation of the lectures was perhaps not entirely objective because some of my classmates used to tease me about my Orlando! I often wondered where he was and what job he was holding.

After my departure to Delhi, I heard indirectly from some common friends that he had left the college to join a new job. When I returned, in those lonely and miserable months, I had tried to locate him several times without any success. In an ironic way, my interpretation of classical English literature allowed me to justify my actions. I was the revolutionary, a rebel with a cause though I was not sure about the ideology. I began to see myself as an extreme version of the Ganymede character, taking revenge on an intolerant masculine world. Though many a man cast glances at my direction, I did not survive long term relationships. My father's 'betrayal' of his near and dear ones had left me with a deep resentment against men and commitment was out of the question.

I was feeling the evening chill. I cradled the Heckler & Koch (PSG1) in my arms. I had modified its barrel to shoot M43 7.62x39mm soft nosed bullets and to allow a Bausch and Lomb sniper scope to be mounted on its rear end. Its foldable butt was made of plastic to make it lighter. It even had a flash guard to hide the location of the sniper. Yes, this was my biggest assignment till date. Eliminate the Commissioner, Special Division and strike a big blow for the cause. Contribute significantly towards the process for overthrowing the bourgeoisie with their corrupt ways and love of such silly pastimes like golf. The 'fee' negotiated for this 'kill' was Ten Million Rupees on completion of my assignment, the money would be wired by some bogus export-import agency based in Bangkok, (little did I care where the money came from). I had been able to 'obtain' PAN cards from two of my victims who were businessmen who had not been able to settle their debts with a loan shark. With the stolen identities, I had set up PayPal accounts so that money transfers were camouflaged with supposedly legitimate business transactions. As I sat on the tree, I took a decision that this would be the last job for me. With my 'savings', I could lose myself amongst the teeming millions in some metropolis. The sun was setting slowly, and the colors of copper, bronze and gold gilding the fairways were turning into depressing shades of grey and black. The scene was indeed a reflection of my present state of mind especially with the dusk beginning to set in. It was becoming apparent that I would have to resume my vigil the next day as getting a clear shot would be difficult in the next 10 minutes or so.

I was about to abandon my post when I suddenly made out a golfer on the fairway accompanied by four men who appeared to be security escorts. As they came closer to my vantage point, I could make out that they were equipped with AK47s and also carried Glock pistols and looked fit, alert and well trained. But I knew from experience that all this readiness and alertness would be neutralized by my advantage of surprise. The sun was behind my back and they would be looking directly into the fading but still strong sunlight. My vantage point further allowed that one crucial shot and the rapid getaway. A boundary wall divided the forest and this part of the course. This would further delay the pursuit and give me time to cut through the dense pine forests, jump on the Yamaha motorbike and vanish into one of the numerous localities of Mawlai Village.

Yes! I had done my planning well. After detailed inquiries, it was revealed that the target was almost inaccessible. He was too well guarded both at home and office. I was told that he belonged to some Federal Civil Service and was quite senior in the bureaucratic hierarchy. I further learnt that he was a bachelor which made my assignment all that harder. No market outings with his family. No regular social engagements. However, I got my lucky break when after some detective work I was able to confirm that he played golf almost every day in the same golf course that I was familiar with! However, for obvious security reasons, he would sometimes play in the evening and in the morning on other days. Since his routine was deliberately unplanned, I had positioned myself for three days but he failed to turn up . . .

The target of my attention was still holding on to his golf club looking happy with himself. I had acquired sufficient golf knowledge to see that his drive was an excellent one, the ball landing on an area near the 100 yards marker stone. This was a par 4hole, about 400 yards in length.

I was about to end his existence and his present state of contentment once and for all. My hatred for golf and all golf players further steeled my resolve. I made sure that the safety selector was in the 'off' mode. Its clacking noise when moved had led to the untimely demise of many a sniper from Vietnam to the Congo. I raised my weapon and peered through the scope . . . 400 yards . . . 350,325 was the sure distance. I visualized the impending scenario. A head shot, the body drop, death struggle and 'bye bye', Mr. Home Commissioner. He approached within range and his face suddenly became distinguishable in the dying light. I curled my finger around the trigger and before I squeezed of the shot, I took a final look at the face of the hated enemy.

'Alas the slings and arrows of outrageous fortune . . . It was the face of my old English teacher!

A TANGLED WEB
(One Moment in Time)

The sunset displayed its magnificent and panoramic best to the two golfers sitting at the outdoor bar of the KGA clubhouse and complemented their mood of utter contentment. They were halfway through their second Chivas Regal whisky and despite playing all 18 holes of the splendid KGA Golf Course, did not feel the aftereffects of aches and pains generally associated with middle age. The splendid view from this vantage point framed by the lush green surroundings could not be found anywhere else in Bangalore. Not even the persistent mosquitoes still buzzing around despite the fact that the swamp had ceased to exist and was now the impressive 18-hole course could disturb the sense of quiet satisfaction of the two golfers. They had both played the perfect round, much below their common handicap of 12 over par and won handsomely from their fellow competitors, two coffee planters who had refused the offer of a consolation drink and scurried home presumably to lick their wounds.

The taller of them, Mr. Ranjeet Row was in a reflective mood. He did not look his 50 odd years. Though he was balding and his goatee was streaked with grey, the years sat lightly on him as it generally did for all those persons who belonged to the dollar billionaire club. He was the CEO of an international

IT corporation, which had not only weathered the recent economic downturn but was also one of the few whose share value had even appreciated. In fact, from where he was sitting, Row could read the signboard on his flagship building located near the new city bypass. 'MATRIX SOLUTIONS' read the neon letters. He pointed it out proudly though without condescension to his close friend and companion, Mr. Arvan Lang who was visiting from Shillong on some official work. Lang was the same age but more thickset in built and his soft features hinted at a mixed Khmer Mongolian origin. Both of them had studied in the same college in New Delhi but their careers had taken them in different directions. Row was now an innovator in computer technology where as Mr. Lang had joined the Civil Service. Despite this difference in income, interests and addresses, their old friendship and love of golf were ties that bound. For them golf was a game which they perceived as being a cut above the rest because it did not need to be umpired or refereed. The player himself kept the score and golfers all around the world were expected to uphold the standards of the game in a gentlemanly manner.

"You know, Lang", began Row . . . Lang took a long sip from his glass and readied himself for a long anecdote. He recalled the good old times in college when they had got bored cramming for their M.A. exams; and instead spent many a night in their hostel room, with their cerebral senses considerably heightened with prohibited substances supplied by an acquaintance from Manali, listening to Jimi Hendrix, Santana, the Who, Led Zeppelin and other guitar gods.

Row was a legendary storyteller and could exaggerate without detracting from the plausibility of his seemingly bottomless stock of yarns. His narrative of his experiences as a sadhu in the Himalayas when he was doing his First Year BA Degree would leave everyone spell bound. There was his story about a time when he hitchhiked to Kerala with only a hundred rupees. After shacking up with a German girl for some months, he got bored and along with a hippie friend had stowed away on a dhow smuggling liquor to U.A.E. and entered the kingdom without any valid papers. Row had finally reached Sweden and made a living as a palmist. Suffice it to say that he had never read a single palm in his life before and did not have a clue about astrology. Arrested by the authorities for residing in the country without the necessary documents, he had been deported back to India. He claimed that he had got himself apprehended as he had become homesick and did not have the money to return. He also claimed that he was getting tired of the close attentions of a well endowed student who doubled up as a masseur in order to earn her pocket money.

Lang as a good friend however believed that this bohemian existence of his best friend in his formative years had molded him into a formidable individual who was uncompromising in matters where values such as honesty and equity were concerned. Though he was happy with the success achieved by Row, he was more proud of the integrity of his best friend. They had shared the same ideals in their formative years but he, Lang, was now no better than the politicians he served. No, you could not say that he was corrupt but his overlooking of a series of acts of commission given his seniority in the bureaucracy made him feel like an accessory to many a crime, albeit a passive one. Row on the other hand was the 'captain of his fate, the master of his soul'. In a world where reputed institutions were becoming frayed and where icons in different places were exposed with feet of clay, Row, at least for Lang was one icon whose honour was held in high esteem and who defied the existing political corporate order.

This opinion was further grounded on the fact that all Matrix employees were shareholders of the company and profits and losses were proportionately shared. No Matrix Solutions worker had ever been fired and very few had quit, which was rare in an industry with a reputation of having the highest employee turnover. The company was a pioneer in computer operating systems. Its latest offering the Megalith OS was one of the latest cutting edge offerings, and was having the same worldwide impact like its Android counterpart. It was now widely used as a software platform for Samsung Smart mobile phones. Though having been introduced recently, this product was driving up the share prices of the company and making it into a world player. Very soon, Lang was convinced; it would be overtaking even Info-Tel for world market share in this particular area.

His companion tapped his arm and jerked him out of his reverie. Row was saying that even though he believed that a man's existence was pre-destined, there were some defining moments or moment, which could shape the course and career of an individual's life. The final destination of course would be the same but the contours of one's existence; physiological less than psychological perhaps, could be affected by the incident. Row opined, "It's how you react and take a decision in that moment or incident which is significant. Even taking no decision is a decision in itself, It's the choice that we have; Ah!, Lang; the power of choice, the original and constant burden of mankind . . . to eat or not to eat; to do or not to do . . . to love or not to love? That is the question."

Lang quickly responded "Row, such things happen to all of us. I remember when I was in two minds about marrying my wife . . . we belonged to different religions and the compatibility problem was always uppermost in my mind. It took almost three years for me to make my decision. Then if you recall, I had that almost fatal accident and her devotion and commitment during my recuperative period convinced me of her intentions. Now I have no regrets. My two daughters are doing well and my wife is very happy with her teaching in a college".

Row conceded this point partially. "My friend", he said, "Granted, but in your case, you were not forced or required to make an instantaneous decision. You had adequate time to examine whether it was in line with your values, morals and most important, your honour. In this instance I am talking about a decision, which when reflected upon arguably compromises your very ethics, your mindset, and your values. The point I am making is that there are times when you need to take a split second decision, where you do not have the time to ponder and introspect. I have almost come to the conclusion that in these cases the decision taken in that moment in time could be on the face of it, highly significant. Significant in that, in the context of that defining moment, the decision would appear to be the logical one and where you think there are no serious ramifications. But, in the aftermath, the decision forces you to look hard into your soul and answer the question whether you have been true to yourself and all you thought you stood for. And after it all, you wonder whether you took the right decision. Regret and remorse is followed swiftly with self-justification. Then you wonder, why do I have to justify to myself? I see that I have lost you. Let me clarify further with my own real life incident.

"You remember", Row said, "When I was going through a bad patch about ten years ago and even you had helped me out with some financial assistance. I had just started to take golf seriously then to build up a network . . . I was making good progress and building up business contacts. However, on one morning I was witness to an incident and my subsequent role in it which I still think about. It happened on this very golf course. If you look towards the 9th hole there, you can see a water hazard built on the right of the fairway to punish a wayward drive. We were competing in a Pro-Am tournament organized by a major cigarette company when tobacco sponsorship was still legitimate. Now, winning this competition was considered by everyone as a major achievement, especially for passionate amateurs like us. Even more important, it could open many doors in the corporate world and could provide that all important break which is so essential for expanding a business.

Well, my fellow player at that time was the CEO of the Indian subsidiary of an international bank. I think it was the Sinclair Bank. His name does not matter now. I had just hit out a wayward ball from those willow trees; they are thicker now of course, when I saw this CEO fellow in front of me taking out a ball from his pocket and dropping it on the secondary rough. It was obvious that he had driven his first ball into the thicket and could not find it. And as you know a lost ball carries a two stroke penalty on the score for the hole. He saw me doing it but pretended as if I was not there. Suffice it to say that the blighter won the tournament by one stroke and I was the runner-up. Now, why did I take the decision to keep mum? Why did I compromise with myself?"

The light was fading fast and most of the greens and fairways had merged with the darkness. The scenery took on a grayish confusing color and indeed it seemed to externalize the state of Lang's present frame of mind. Lang suddenly felt the whisky affecting his head and could not answer Row's question directed at him. Row interpreted his silence as a signal to carry on. He said, "You always praise my ethics and values and my uncompromising attitude to any wrongdoing. Yes, I and I have tried to keep the flag flying. I could have reported the cheating to the golf captain and that would have been the end of the matter insofar as everyone was concerned. That cheat would have kept away from the golf club for a month or so and by then the whole incident would have been almost forgotten. But for me, it was not as simple as that. I needed a soft loan from that man! My company was almost going under and my credibility had eroded to the extent that all banks had shut their doors on my face. I had invested every penny I had into the company. My condoning of that cheating gave me access to a line of credit from Sinclair Bank. On the face of it my decision to keep quiet did not harm anyone. From then on, everything fell naturally into place. That chap is somewhere in the U.S. and holding a very senior position in Citibank. Now as you can see, I have also arrived! I have become a pillar of the corporate community, well respected and popular for my philanthropic causes and handsome contributions to local charities. But sometimes I wake up in the middle of the night and ask myself whether that decision to keep quiet was worth it. I feel that I have surrendered to the corrupt system, where cheating and conniving is justified as a means to an end. I know now that that bloody banker had had the foresight to realize that I would not squeal on him because of my predicament. Now more than ever, when I think about that incident, I feel that the difference between those politicians and me is now only in degree and not in kind. What do you think?"

Lang again could not answer . . . Shakespeare was right . . . 'What a tangled web we weave', he mused. The image he had consistently held of one of his heroes, nay one of his icons had just disintegrated in front of him . . . A lighthouse of certainty which had withstood the waves of change for so long was now disintegrating in front of him. He slapped at a persistent mosquito and suddenly felt his backache acting up. He suddenly believed that even his beloved golf game, an anchor of constancy in an increasingly materialistic and uncertain world would soon be no better than any other game-open to deal fixing and crass commercialization. Neither the noise of the rush hour traffic nor the roar of an Air India jet as it took off from the nearby airport could distract him from the fact that his iconic friend was a mere mortal after all.

THE SPIRIT OF
BEN HOGAN

The Dunlop 1-iron sat forlornly in the long wooden cabinet displaying second hand clubs for sale. Every other day, Mani, the barman-cum-supervisor, would place some item or the other there for sale and sales were usually steady. But even the most disinterested observer would have noticed that the long iron remained unnoticed and untouched. Many young aspiring Tiger Woods would firstly go for the drivers, and then the utility woods; the fives, or the sevens and no one it seemed had any use for the solitary long iron.

The display cabinets were located almost parallel to the bar in the old extension of the still older club house which had been newly renovated courtesy of a government grant made possible by a golf playing bureaucrat who had taken up golf. This very bureaucrat, Mr. Arvan Lang was enjoying a bottle of Budweiser beer with his batch mate in the civil service, Mr. Ashok Kumar a fellow golfing enthusiast from the Rajasthan Cadre and posted in the Ministry of Rural Development at New Delhi. Though Lang and Kumar were not really friendly during their training in the IAS Training Academy due to their different personalities, their frequent meetings in regional and national golf tournaments organized primarily for civil servants by the Ministry of Personnel and Training to promote 'esprit de corps' did at least ensure that they fraternized more often than not. However, in this instance, Kumar had come ostensibly on an official tour to the state to review the centrally sponsored MNRGA schemes. In fact he also wanted to avail of a chance to play golf in a naturally air conditioned golf course. It was the middle of June, the pre-monsoon time and whilst searing heat and acute water shortages was affecting the large parts of the country, the good citizens of Shillong town luxuriated in their sylvan and salubrious surroundings.

Amidst the inevitable post mortem and the 'ifs' that followed the conclusion of every keenly contested round, Kumar's attention was drawn to the old 1-iron and soon, he and his companion began remembering about the singular recovery shots executed with long irons and which had become a part of golf folklore. In particular they recalled the incredible 3rd shot the great Ben Hogan executed on the 18th fairway at Merion Golf Club. Pennsylvania. It was the 72nd hole of the 1950 US Open and Hogan, the eventual winner with legs still bandaged from the near fatal car crash needed to make 'par' to make it to the playoff the next day. Ahead of Hogan was an unbelievably narrow fairway of almost 250 yards in length terminating in a tiny green made lethally fast with four days of bright sun and protected by a monstrous bunker to the front right of the green. Hogan extracted his 1-iron and summoning his last ounces of energy, struck the ball into the heart of the green and made 'par'! The three way playoff was easily won by Hogan. And the story became an inspiration for millions of sportsmen all over the world.

"You will not believe me, boss," said Lang, 'but that 1-iron out there played a similarly significant part though not of the Hogan magnitude in the life of one of our fellow golfers here. This fellow whom I will not name (Let us call him Mr. Roy) was in fact a member of our sister service who has since resigned. He is now making large amounts of money on the professional Asian Golf circuit. But till about 5 years ago, he was on the verge of penury. He had deserted his wife and his meager pension was used to pay off the alimony. The only thing he had going was his love of golf and he was simply going nowhere. He tried to qualify several times for the Asian Tour from the Qualifying (Q) School usually held in Jaipur but failed in all his attempts. One couldn't blame him of course. You of all people will know that the Jaipur golf course becomes a desert in summer! Our friend stagnated in Shillong and his games were now confined to betting with whoever came along. At one point he even took up coaching but the universal belief as you yourself have once told me is that a good player does not make a good coach. And he was very good'.

Kumar signaled Mani for another beer. He reserved his comments as he replenished his friend's glass an act which had briefly interrupted the anecdote. Lang continued, 'I often played with Mr. Roy and I knew about his career and his continuous problems with politicians. I could understand his compulsions for taking premature retirement. He was of the belief that he had another option in life despite the fact that he belonged to a premier service. I am sure you of all people will understand why'. Kumar did understand. When they joined the IAS, they believed they were like the philosopher knights of Aristotelian Greece; motivated to serve society with compassion and impartiality. They believed that they could change the system and make a tangible difference. Before they could realize it, all their visions of development unraveled before their eyes. The nexus between some unscrupulous and self-aggrandizing members of their service with businessmen and politicians existed before their entry into the government and would continue after their exit. In almost every conversation, they would discuss about unfulfilled potential and the frustration of being sidelined in a system that favored mostly cronyism and corruption.

Their golf fortunately provided an escape route from this frustration of not being able to generate tangible outcomes and being stymied by minefields of corruption and hidden agenda of bad governance. The game arguably provided a dimension to their life where skills and commitment were instantly rewarded with appropriate outcomes. This contrasted sharply with the culture prevalent in their workplace. It provided a cathartic outlet though only on weekends. They often discussed the option of quitting but they lacked the skills and courage to leave their comfort zones and consoled themselves with the thought that better days lay ahead. Kumar said that he admired the courage of the man who could take golf up as a full time profession and give up all the perks and privileges of government service.

Lang continued with his narration about how the subject of his story had almost become a derelict person avoided by all his friends until fate dealt him an ace of spades! Kumar was told that the subject of his friend's narrative got a chance to participate in a competition organized for aspiring professionals so as to allow them to enter professional tournaments. It transpired that due to the unrelenting heat in other parts of India, some five years ago the Indian Golf Association temporarily shifted the venue of the Q School to this very course. Lang recounted on how Mr. Roy began to practice without even taking a break for meals. He recalled the sight of Mr. Roy chipping and putting for long hours on the practice green in pitch black conditions, with the only illumination provided by scores of candles placed strategically on the perimeter of the practice green.

Lang carried on with his anecdote after he had downed his beer with a flourish to lend some dramatic effect to his story. 'The big day' he said, 'finally came perhaps a little too quick for our friend. I followed Mr. Roy throughout the entire round of 18 holes. Over forty golfers aspiring to qualify for the Asian Tour had entered the fray. The qualifying round was set over 18 holes and the qualifying cut was set at one under the course par of 70. In layman terms, a player would need to achieve a score of '69', which was quite difficult considering the topography of the Shillong Golf course with its angled fairways and small greens. Our friend was now confident of qualifying. After all, it was his home course and I recall one of his friends in particular; a certain Colonel Mishra who often commented that Roy could recognize every blade of grass on the course.

"Mr. Roy uncharacteristically made a one over par on the first nine holes" Lang informed, "but, I could see that he was still confident in making the qualifying cut as it was his home course. And in any case it was common knowledge that he had frequently carded a three under round or better on the comparatively easier back nine. So, till the 16th hole, Kumar, the going was good. His game was holding up as expected and his card read at two under par with three birdies made on the trot on the 14th, 15th and 16th holes. His other two fellow competitors were already reconciled to missing the cut. But on the penultimate hole that is the 17th hole, which was a par four, I felt that Lady Luck deserted him.

I watched him crunch his ball and hit a booming 270 yard drive. But to my dismay his second shot bounced off the fairway and onto the adjacent trees, and he was forced to take a one penalty drop. With his composure completely shredded, he dropped one stroke on what was supposed to be a routinely easy hole. His score now stood at one under! Mr. Roy now stood on the eighteen tee box, knowing that all he needed was a 'par'! I could sense the tension surrounding the man but no one would imagine the turbulence in his mind".

Kumar's level of interest became more aroused. He could visualize the thoughts of Lang's friend. 'A par'; in itself an ordinarily meaning and simple sounding three letter verb. But in the context of the contest, this target, this 'par' if achieved would open the windows of opportunity into an exciting, new and certainly a better world. He glanced out of the window and took in the contours of the 18th fairway. It looked relatively simple. And he had made a par on this par-4 hole. But hang on, he thought. Come to think of it, he saw that not only was the fairway narrow, but it sloped steeply to the right bounded on the left by a public road linking the adjacent market place and the road leading to the State Police Training Centre. He had been informed that balls landing on this road are declared as out of bounds (O.B.). And he noticed that on the right of the fairway, there was a line of old pine trees solid and rugged in their permanence. Even a new golfer could discern that a ball striking or landing at the foot of these sentinels spelt trouble for the player as they would obscure his sight of the green and literally obstruct the line of the ball.

Lang again invigorated by another swig of Budweiser beer came to the conclusion of the story. He said, 'I could feel for Mr. Roy as he took his stance behind the ball on the tee box and wiggled the club head of his driver. I could see the tension oozing out of every pore of his body. I could read his mind as he mentally visualized his shot, the arc of the ball and the landing safely beyond the trees. I could actually sense the tightness of his muscles and the turmoil of his mind. I could see that he wanted to play a safety shot and avoid going O.B. That was his undoing, I think. In going too far right, his ball struck one of the pine trees and the ball ricocheted back behind one of the pine trees onto the adjacent first fairway. After his second recovery shot onto the 18th fairway, he was left with a 200 yard plus recovery shot onto the 18th green guarded by giant sand traps on both the front sides of the green. He needed to guarantee that this third shot would enable him to putt for a par. I could see the man virtually at the end of his tether! His caddy handed him a three wood club. But no! A visibly swaying Mr. Roy spurned the outstretched hand and plucked out the 1-iron, which you see now displayed in front of you. His ball landed a good two feet from the cup. That final putt provided more high voltage drama and Mr. Roy took a very long time in lining up his ball. But he did make his 'par'! The rest is history . . .

THE HAND OF GOD
(The Silver Bullet)

Hello! My name is Mr. Digvijai Singh, formerly a lieutenant colonel with the Indian Army. You may have seen me playing professional golf in one of the many PGA tournaments being screened in the Ten Golf Channel. My career is closely followed by all those golf aficionados who often marvel at my achievements. In fact, my manager has been regularly forwarding me all the blog queries as to how I arrived at this enviable position despite my Indian Military background. I have chosen not to reveal the facts as the situation has added a fair bit of allure to my personality. Now with the thought of retirement from the professional tour circuit constantly on my mind, I feel that the right time has arrived for me to clear the mystery and to explain as to how a 'silver bullet' changed my destiny . . .

I still can remember that dreadful day nearly two decades ago, when I woke up in the Research & Referral Military Hospital with an AK-47 bullet still lodged in my upper left arm. The surgeons could not remove the bullet or they would have needed to amputate almost the entire arm. They had since removed another two bullets from my abdomen. The surgeons said that I was lucky it was not the soft nosed variety or I would have lost the entire hand if not my life. But it was no consolation as some nerves had been damaged. I could not straighten my wrist. I could not even rotate it and it was frozen at an unnatural angle. A silver lining was that my right hand was totally untouched and functioned normally.

I never really saw the faceless sniper who would have such a 'shattering' effect on my existence. I could well imagine his situation; probably unsure of his ideology and his future, he could have been one of those thousands of unemployed youths in the Northeast. A social scientist would perhaps have categorized him as a product of short-term government policies and an archaic education system that was out of touch with the aspirations of the rural communities and in the bargain unknowingly subverted youthful exuberance and natural genius.

But, I did not care about such social circumstances that could have created him and his kind. In those long lonely months in a hospital ward, I constantly cursed this anonymous youth and his entire tribe for snuffing out my raison d'être. I would have been better off dead. I wallowed in self-pity. My promising professional career was now ruined. Everyone in the army, peers and superiors alike used to comment on my potential and praise my single-minded commitment to my career. I had been the top cadet from the NDA, Pune and commissioned into the elite Guards regiment. I was drafted into the Special Armed Forces and underwent guerilla warfare and counter insurgency training in the Counter-insurgency Warfare School (CIWS), Mizoram. After six months of relentless training with members of the SAS, I was unleashed by my minders. Countless encounters in the steamy jungles of the Northeast, dawn raids against Afghan militants in the Kashmir morass, had left me battle hardened, unscathed and rising up the regimental ladder in double quick time.

In fact I was due for my own command when fate dealt me this unkind blow. It was all downhill thereafter. I was medically downgraded and posted in a desk job in somewhere in the steamy plains of Western Bihar. The change in my life inevitably led to the midnight binges, endless quarrels with the wife, and the final showdown. Divorce proceedings were started and I was separated from my two sons. My prolonged single miserable existence all pointed to the one and only inevitable end. I had the death wish and day by day, even my closest friends avoided me like the plague. Due to my outstanding record, I was not cashiered by the army and a kind general posted in Fort William and who had served as the Director in the Vairengte School during my training there thought that a change of environment would help me overcome my depression pulled strings for my deputation to the N.C.C.'s regional office in Shillong. As the saying goes, 'a change is always good . . .' and maybe that unknown sage got it right in my case. Perhaps, due to the change in climate and company, I took to playing golf regularly with an affable bureaucrat, whose name was Arvan Lang in the breathtakingly beautiful century old golf course there. I had never played golf before thinking that I would take up the game seriously after my retirement. I had always held the view that the game of golf was for the pensioner and the elderly. Squash, tennis and badminton used to be my favorite sports. But my injury put paid to these healthy pursuits and now the game, which I had often belittled, would eventually prove to be my lifesaver.

Suffice it to say that I became a natural. My erstwhile pursuits of strenuous racket games came in handy not only for timing but also for hand and eye coordination. But the singular thing that amazed all the local golf coaches was the fact that I did not need to be taught how to cock my wrist and bend my elbow for achieving the 'picture perfect swing' so essential for spin, maximum loft and distance. At moment of impact my left wrist straightened automatically. I was told that all these movements and motions had to be drilled into all aspiring golfers, as they are not natural. It was an accepted fact that for all right handed persons, the right hand would always take the lead. But in golf, it was the left that was the predominant lever. In fact, I was further informed that this movement was arguably the biggest impediment to the improvement of any golfer as they determined the shape and balance of the swing. But in an ironic manner, these movements of cocking the wrist, bending of the elbow etc, were natural to my unconventional left hand. In record time, I became a scratch player and was winning amateur tournaments around the country. Then the professional tournament touring circuit beckoned and I went to the national Q-school and qualified to play in professional tournaments at my first attempt. I began winning golf tournaments in cities like Calcutta and Delhi. Within a relatively short span of time, I had crossed the oceans to the Land of Dreams. As it was too late in my life to join the regular PGA tour, I qualified to play in the Seniors Tour. I soon became the No 1 in career winnings and even won the Seniors Grand Slam in one calendar year.

Suffice it to say that I am now reunited with my wife and two sons and we are settled in California near the famous Pebble Beach Golf Course. All thanks to one 'silver' bullet which failed to find its true mark one hot summer's day long ago, in the blue hills of the Barail Mountain Range.

You, the discerning reader could perhaps attribute my destiny literally to my 'Hand' of God!

OF MICE AND MEN

'Well, you may not believe this, son, but around this time about a year ago, I was unwittingly responsible for preventing the outbreak of World War III and the destruction of the major portion of the civilized world as we know it now. And it will probably be the only time when I truly was grateful for making a wayward shot'. The speaker was making this statement to a younger man who was relaxing with a beer after playing a full round of golf on a warm April day at the Delhi Golf Club. The sheer effrontery coupled with the incongruity of this outrageous statement would have drawn howls of protest and 'shut ups' from less polite mortals that would in all probability sent the elderly looking speaker scurrying for cover.

But his younger male companion was too polite to ask his older companion to shut up and simply stifled a yawn. His politeness perhaps derived from showing some respect to the older man. The young man had been brought up in the traditional Indian way where showing deference to elders was an important part of etiquette. Despite his advanced age, and a voice rendered hoarse by constant smoking, the old man had an air of authority and there was an aura of quiet dignity about him. He had one of those faces which people normally associate with 'friendly uncles' who often play the sheet anchor role for troubled young nephews. Looking at the young man, the onlooker would not have noted anything out of the ordinary. He would have noticed the sun tanned face, the athletic frame, the muscular forearms and the broad shoulders all pointing to the fact that the young man was a competent, perhaps a professional golfer. What was partially concealed by the golf cap however were the eyes-opaque like the waters of a deep shaded pool hinting at some unknown aspect in the character?

The two men were now almost alone in the favorite watering hole, 'The Pub' located on the terrace of the Annexe Building. There were two other persons in the far end of the lounge. One of them was a former Minister who to perhaps camouflage his insecurity behaved in a bossy manner that bordered on the offensive. It was an open secret amongst most of the members that that this politician had managed his membership when he was still in power from the discretionary quota allotted to the Ministry of Urban Development. Other golfers were leaving or had left for their homes and the magnificent view of the undulating fairways and lush greens was slowly losing ground to the gathering summer gloom. The young man thought about an excuse and making good his escape. The shadows began to rapidly lengthen, but the cold Corona beer tasted like ambrosia. He was already on his 4th bottle (?) and at this rate he would have to watch his waistline and maybe fit in some games of squash just to supplement his weekly golf round. His companion's monologue interrupted his stream of consciousness, and he forced himself to listen on stifling his impulse to leave. Anyway, he had no pressing engagement . . . he had time to kill; his wife was surely busy with her all Sunday social program and his two children were staying with their maternal grandmother. He realized with a pang of remorse that he was getting increasingly isolated from his family. But such was the call of 'duty'. He would make it up to them when he retired for good. All his wife knew was what he told her. She was a good woman, silently accepting his long absences and his explanation that his consultancy job entailed long tours overseas. He sometimes wished that he had followed his elder cousin's footsteps and become a civil servant. But he could sense that Arvan Lang was getting increasingly frustrated with the hidden agenda and political compulsions of public service and was talking frequently about quitting. Well, there was no frustration with his occupation. He had been an average student and was allergic to all forms of desk work. He therefore welcomed and took up the tough challenges associated with the job. So retirement could not be contemplated, not now, not even in the near future, when he still had the energy and the motivation. He would make it up to his family when the time was right!

Listening to the older man he learnt that his name was I. R. Dass. He had retired some years back from some security service, and because of his stature had been nominated as the Golf Captain of the Club. Apart from this factor, the old man was still a very good golfer. He followed Dass's finger pointing out a tall building in the near distance and who was saying; 'If you look across over those trees, you can see the Oberoi Hotel overlooking the course . . . You would recall that it was chosen as the venue for that epic summit a year ago, between our country and Pakistan. That summit was timely, I say! We were nearly at war with each other over the never ending Kashmir issue. The hawks on both sides of the divide were nuclear trigger happy, and God forbid, if anything had happened to the Pakistani President here, New Delhi would have been wiped out in the first offensive, and vice versa for Islamabad" Dass took a sip from his whisky and taking his companion's silence as a signal of acquiescence carried on . . . "Security arrangements was unprecedented and succumbing to extreme pressure from the U.S., a no war pact was signed along with substantial trade agreements including the resumption of road and rail links between the two countries. The media hailed the results as the best development in bilateral relations between our two countries since the Shimla Agreement. A road map was drawn up to carry the process forward and everybody breathed a sigh of relief. The General or the President; call him what you will, was due to leave the next day".

The younger man remembered the meeting of the two leaders and remembered only the TV channels and newspapers extolling the success and hailing the strategic significance of the summit. He was now even more convinced that the old man was being ignored by other members and did not want to drink his whisky in solitude. His tall tales were obviously a ploy of ensuring some company. He got up to leave but the seriousness of his companion's expression held him back. And the beer tasted even better. He signaled to the barman for another Corona and a repeat round for his companion.

Dass touched his arm to indicate his thanks and carried on with his story. He was saying 'But the general postponed his departure by one day. Why? To play a round of golf on this very golf course. He was a golf aficionado with a seven handicap, and was aware of the reputation and challenge of the Lodhi Golf Course. As I was the Golf Captain, I was instructed to arrange the four-ball—the President, the Indian Defense Minister, the Chief of Army Staff and myself.

The day turned out to be perfect for golf', Dass recalled. 'A brisk breeze blowing from a north by northeasterly direction brought relief to the golfers playing in the warm summer's day. Peacocks were serenading each other and partridges were wallowing in the shallow waters of the lakes. The Army Chief and the Defense Minister were in the opposing two-man team and I was partnering El Presidente. It was a match play format where the best individual score was taken into consideration. All four of us were on our game and after 17 holes it was a deadlock and the match was all square. The final result hinged on the outcome of the 18th hole and El Presidente for the first time in the morning began to look tense. I guess more than winning the wager of Rs 10000, it was the bragging rights of putting 'one over' his Indian guests'.

Dass's voice got hoarser as he carried on with the narration. 'The drama started on the dogleg 18th par five hole' he informed, 'which you can see here through the window in front of you. My countrymen having won the 17th hole which had squared the contest had the honour of teeing off first. Both of their drives split the fairway in two, though they sacrificed length for accuracy. Any errant drive, whether hook or slice would entail even at best, a penalty drop as the tangle of roots and shrubs forming the undergrowth of the forest on both sides of the fairway ruled out the possibility of any recovery shot.

El Presidente placed his ball and checked his line. He was well aware of the importance of hitting a long drive. He saw that the Army Chief and the Defense Minister would need a minimum of three shots to reach the green. Faced with the situation of reaching the green in two shots, victory was his. With the condescending attitude and over confidence that is the characteristic of many dictators, he gave his ball a mighty whack. Alas, he sliced viciously and his ball landed square in the middle of the trees on the right of the fairway. Who was that sage who had proclaimed that all men are equal before golf? All his hopes now rested on my old shoulders. A deliberate bad shot by me would have all but surely handed over the bragging rights to India.

All eyes or six of them to be precise if you excluded the caddies and the horde of security men were boring into me. I felt that my patriotism was on the line. I dearly wanted to muff my shot for the sake of my country. But for me, my young friend, golf is a gentleman's game, and not to be mixed up with politics and gamesmanship. I forced my bile down and concentrated on my swing. I knew that I had to hit a fade so I closed my stance a fraction. When my club made contact with the ball, I knew I had connected with the 'sweet spot' of my driver, and I was sure that the ball would turn from left to right at the end of the dogleg. With my knowledge of my home course, I had already mentally selected my club for the second shot into the green. I began to imagine the unconditional and eternal gratitude of my partner. I could see his expression changing from stormy to sunlight. Suddenly for no apparent reason, my ball veered off course in mid flight and landed on the forest bordering the left hand side of the fairway. To cut a long story short, we lost the hole and the match, and along with it my chance to be a lifelong honorary citizen of our neighboring country. The President did not even shake my hand as he stormed off the course, and he never bothered to contact me again. I couldn't blame him, of course!"

Dass said "You must be now wondering why my ball veered off to the left. O.K! You may find it hard to believe this. Let me explain! I sent my caddy to retrieve the ball immediately after the dictator had departed. To my surprise it had a shallow furrow, dark grey in color which had almost erased the brand name. It was a Nike ball promoted by Tiger Woods, expensive, no doubt, but one of a dozen brought by my wife on her last trip overseas. The mark was singular in shape and my past experience with guns made me suspect that my ball smelt faintly of cordite. After mulling over the mystery for some time, I got it analyzed by a former colleague working in the Forensic Lab in the Delhi Police. His tests confirmed my suspicions that it had been impacted by a stray bullet? After weeks of pondering, I finally arrived at a conclusion that you may find hard to believe . . .'

The young man was now all ears and his beer stood neglected and warm in front of him. Dass's offer of another bottle was politely declined and he continued; 'I would presume that as my ball was travelling in the intended direction, it was accidentally deflected by a bullet fired by a sniper holed up somewhere on the top floor of Oberoi Hotel. He must have had a clear line of sight on the 18th tee-box. I would again presume that this gunman could have been a fanatic belonging to some rabid fundamentalist or could have been a mercenary driven by a profit motive. The would-be assassin must have got away as there was no incident or disaster reported then. But I am sure of one thing; the bullet would have found its mark if my ball had not got in the way!"

The younger man got up, his impassive face revealing no expression or feelings. Inside though, he was all frustration and anger at the thought of all his planning and time being wasted . . . he thought about the long hours of practice with the Heckler & Koch (PSG1) rifle. He recalled the effort needed to reserve the room in Oberoi Hotel using fictitious identity papers and the expenditure involved. Fuck! He inwardly cursed; the vagaries of chance! No man could accurately predict the outcome of even the most meticulous planned operation. Shakespeare had indeed got it right when he had written that 'God lays to rest the best laid plans of mice and men'. Hadn't he read in the papers that this President had cheated death five times? Unbeknownst to the President and to the public, he had cheated death for the sixth time in Delhi. But the young man would make sure there would be no seventh time; no golf ball would thwart his designs the next time. He could not afford to allow his reputation of being the 'best' in the 'Agency' be affected by such a major failure. The President was visiting neighboring Bangladesh in the near future for a SAARC conference. The assassin would have an opportunity again to set his record right in Dhaka. After all, that mid air collision was a one in a trillion chance!

HEAVEN AND EARTH

'VATICAN BENDS ITS OWN RULES' screamed the news in several international newspapers, and dominated the news in all TV networks as word spread all over about the beatification of Mother Serena who had passed away in her late nineties. The good Mother, who originally hailed from Slovakia was a recipient of innumerable international awards including the Nobel Peace Prize and was regarded widely as a beacon of hope and inspiration for countless millions. She was revered for her social work amongst the lepers community during her 70 years spent in the Indian subcontinent. The inhabitants of the only hill station town in Sri Lanka, Nuwara Eliya nestled at 7000 feet above sea level In particular, were abuzz with excitement as the good mother had spent almost her last days there in the landmark hotel, 'The El Grande'. In fact, Mother Serena had come to this hilly town to spend some time after her visit to the famous Christian shrine at Adam's Peak in the nearby district. And yes, it was in this hotel that she had reportedly performed a miracle. (She had died soon after in the city of Calcutta).

As reported by the newspapers, an elderly man who was born blind had regained his sight after being blessed by the Mother. And in fact, this miracle was the main factor arguably solely responsible for the impending canonization. Leading international ophthalmologists had certified that this 'blessed' man had been afflicted by congenital blindness for which there was no known cure! It was reported that the blind man had been treated at the best eye hospital in Chennai without any positive outcome.

Coincidentally after her sojourn in this hill station, I had visited Nuwara Eliya for a week, not as a tourist, but as an international observer, for the 2001 parliamentary elections of Sri Lanka. At that point in time, I was posted as the State Election Commissioner in Meghalaya. Along with ten other State Election Commissioners from other parts of India we were selected to observe the election process for the elections in the island. I remember being briefed in New Delhi by the then Chief Election Commissioner, the formidable J. M. Lyngdoh who had directed us to be diligent in our duties and to showcase the efficiency of the Indian electoral system to our hosts. On the contrary, on arrival we were accommodated in the Lanka Oberoi on Galle Road in Colombo for over a week. Our hosts were indeed generous and we were given free runs on all the bars and restaurants in this seven star hotel. However, our outdoor movements were restricted by the frequent curfews called due to the civil war raging then on the island. Briefing by the election officials of Sri Lanka was short and to the point. We observed that by and large, the Sri Lankan Election Commission was quite easy going and preparations were not as claustrophobic as the ones made by the Indian Election Commission for conducting polls in our country.

Three days prior to the designated polling day, I set out by road to Nuwara Eliya along with my security escorts. Despite the distance being only less than 200 kilometers. It took almost the entire day to reach our destination due to the frequent stoppages at the army roadblocks all along the route. In spite of these hindrances, I thoroughly enjoyed the drive. I remember travelling on the Hatton road enjoying the view from the St Clare Tea Estate. The economy of the district is based mainly on tourism and the sprawling tea gardens that have made Ceylonese tea internationally renowned. My hosts being very generous had put me up in the same hotel where Mother Serena had spent her last days. The El Grande Hotel built in the Tudor style was a 'white guests only' during colonial days. The rooms were luxurious, the bathrooms impeccable and the cuisine sublime. The icing on this cake was the magnificent 70 par, 5550 meters long 18 holes golf course laid in 1891 lying adjacent and with the 17th fairway running parallel to the driveway of the El Grande hotel. The only partition dividing the grounds was a thick gorse hedge of about 5 feet in height.

Being a keen amateur golfer, I wasted no time in teeing off in front of the impressive clubhouse on the very first morning after my arrival. I must confess now that I did not show due diligence in my observatory duties and was relieved when there were no major incidents to mar the elections. The relaxed behavior of the District Secretary who is the equivalent of our District Collector more than eased my guilty conscience. Anyway returning to the main theme of my narrative, I found the golf course extremely challenging. The majority of the fairways was narrow and hazards too numerous to count. Forests of cypress, acacia and birch dotted the course and woes betide the golfer who sliced or hooked. One had to hit long and straight in order to play a satisfactory round. I was lucky in finding myself a very good caddie, who was a Plantation Tamil.

His name was Miles and his advice was reliable. He even succeeded in curing my slice that had become so subtle that it would have defied even the close attentions of Butch Harmon, if I could have been rich enough to afford the coaching classes. It transpired that Miles had been a gifted golfer, good enough to turn professional, except that he had been singularly unlucky. While caddying for a golfer some three years ago, he had been hit in his wrist when the blighter had hooked his drive. The impact had been so severe that several bones had been broken and the end result was the demise of yet another promising golfer.

Miles then narrated how his bête noir was in fact a regular but the most unpopular member in the course. He was the owner of several tea gardens in the district of Nuvara Eliya and very rich. But he abused the caddies; criss—crossed the course without so much as 'if you please'. His behavior was so boorish that despite his wealth other players avoided him. It was rumored that his wife had left him for a poorer but more affable companion. I could visualize the character of the man and even predict his future life. With no redeeming qualities, he would be negotiating the journey of life with the egoistic belief that everybody could be purchased compounded with a severe attitude problem. Only people wanting to sponge off him would feed his ego and in the end he would be isolated and convinced that the whole world was conspiring against him. He would have died alone and surrounded only by those relatives who were interested in his will. He would be forgotten immediately after his demise with no one to mourn for him or remember him. Miles interrupted my reverie and said if the man weren't so well off, and influential he would have been expelled from the club. He lost an average of 6 balls every round and must have held the world record in hitting balls out of bounds (O.B.s). In fact, he was referred to by other members of the club as Mister OB.

Continuing with his narrative, Miles said that Mr. O.B. had recently shanked his second shot on the 4 par 17th hole so severely that his ball had struck a middle aged gentlemen flush on his temple as he was entering the adjacent El Grand Hotel. It seemed that this unfortunate man was blind. Come to think if it, said Miles, it was the very day when the late Good Mother Serena had granted an audience to the public. Her presence could have very well have saved Mr. O.B. from the wrath of the crowd assembled there. The injured man had been carried into the hotel and subsequently blessed by the Good Mother.

A question suddenly flashed in my mind. "Could it be possible?" I could visualize the blind man being guided to the hotel hoping for a miracle from Mother Serena. Struck by Mr. OB's wayward ball, and disoriented, he would have thought that the end was nigh. Suddenly after being blessed, he must have opened his eyes and seen living colors for the first time. In all probability, the impact of ball on skull could very well have restored his sight.

Shakespeare' famous lines; 'There are more things on heaven and earth, Horatio, than are dreamt of in your philosophy' suddenly became very relevant to me. I had profiled Mr. OB as having no redeeming bone in his body and whose demise would have not been mourned. Yet, unbeknownst to him, and to his peers, he unknowingly performed an act which had far reaching consequences. The salutary effect of his errant golf shot without a shred of doubt led to an outcome which enhanced the symbolical and saintly power of an individual who even after her death, is worshipped as a symbol of hope and grace in an increasingly cynical and disbelieving world.

N.B. As narrated by Mr. Arvan Lang to his colleague during their daily lunch break.

AN ARTICLE OF FAITH

The sunset burnished the emerald green ocean with golden hues and the reflection of sky meeting sea counterpointed the sprawling thatch and timber Colombo clubhouse making it appear like a magical lodge of a fairytale Disney kingdom. Despite the departure of the British almost three score of a century earlier, the club still retained it colonial grandeur. Liveried waiters padded about barefoot taking orders for Sinhalese fusion dishes which were arguably the best in the island. It was cool in Sri Lanka even by May standards the cause being a brisk sea breeze blowing from the West. But the two golfers sitting at the verandah bar of the clubhouse drinking their Glenmorangie single malts were seemingly oblivious of their surroundings. To a casual onlooker, the fairer of them, Mr. Desmond Dash appeared to be the more drunk and vocal of the two. He was the CEO of a software and networking company, (Orchid Software Solutions) based in Skillmans, NJ., and he and his old school friend Mr. Arvan Lang were on a golfing holiday to Sri Lanka. Dash was an inveterate gambler frequenting casinos around the world and betting heavily on the outcome of major golf tournaments such as the Barclays, Deutsche Bank to name a few. And though more lucky than most, there were whispers in the corporate corridors that his fortunes had recently taken a severe beating after the recent FedEx golf tournament held in the splendid but uncompromising 70 par, 7000+ yards, TPC Boston Course in Massachusetts.

"You know, Lang", said Dash. "I was always a believer in the complete dominance of technology in everyday life vis a vis the exaggerated element of luck and divine intervention in our existence. Scientists have achieved spectacular results, for example in missions in outer space, the space shuttles, and the recent experiments on the Boson Particle. Yes, for me the overriding power of technology and science was for me, an article of faith. But, recently, an act of nature if you will has rendered all my notions of technology useless. The outcome of this incident has made a permanent impact on my existence. And that was the cause of my ill luck, and if you will, my loss of faith".

Lang prepared himself mentally for his friend's bad luck story. It seemed that this time, the losses were significant as some business acquaintances had informed him about Dash selling off a major chunk of his holdings in his corporation due to some misfortune. Share prices of the Orchid Corporation were spiraling downwards as skittish investors unloaded their stakes. Till now, Lang was not aware that this situation had been caused because of a failure at match fixing. He was therefore ready to lend his shoulder to his good friend and prepared himself mentally by taking a big swig of the Glenmorangie 18 years old whisky. It was his maiden visit to the island, and he was enjoying the rare single malt, a drink he could never afford with the government salary he was getting. On the other hand, his old classmate, Desmond was one of the shining stars on the IT firmament and till the other day, Bloomberg Inc. had been routinely predicting the rosy investment prospects for the Orchid Corporation.

The company's core business was in chip design. In fact, earlier in the evening, Desmond had been talking about a chip he was about to place on the market which would enable multiple voice and video applications to be hosted on one single platform. He had acquired a legendary reputation in managing to anticipate public demand particularly in the areas of social networking and online gaming. Recently, the company had launched a social network service called 'Birdie' which targeted the million of golfers around the world. What were even more gratifying were the hundreds of jobs the company had created in the underdeveloped region of Northeastern India. Now, Lang wondered, was all this effort and assets going down the drain because of one man's ambition and hunger for even more wealth and power?

His reverie was broken by his companion's voice, continuing with his bad luck story. And the tale he had to tell centered on golf. Dash was saying that in every era, one individual player had invariably dominated the golf world. For example, in the sixties no one could match the prowess of the Great Dane. Then in the seventies it was the Golden Bear. The eighties witnessed the amazing exploits of the Great White Shark. In the nineties and early 2000s, it was the turn of the Tundra Tiger. Presently everybody was talking about the Timber Wolf and his total dominance of the PGA Tour. Desmond whispered that The Wolf was superior to all those past champions. His ability was not entirely due to training and talent and championship qualities, he informed 'sotto voce'.

Lang's interest was aroused and he sat up in his easy chair. Dash continued, 'you recall, Lang, when I had told you about the chip I was about to launch in the market. NASA did the initial groundwork for improving their astronauts' ability to perform complex operations in an outer space environment. I somehow gained access to the software and further developed and designed a product exclusively for the golf market. I had named it the 'Reflex Chip'.

"Now" said Dash, you being a golfer would be aware that golf is arguably the only outdoor game where the reflex aspect does not play a primary role. As you know, old chap, natural hand and eye coordination is inbuilt in all animals and is deployed primarily as a reflex or instinctive reaction. It is a response to a danger or hitting or catching a fast moving object, the lead time between thought and action is very minimal and as is commonly known, successful athletes are blessed with fast reflexes. Reflex and instinct primarily determine and guide the pace and extent, the length and line of the struck object. For example, in games such as cricket, tennis or baseball, the reflex aspect plays a crucial role. And training hones this reflex and talent further enhances it".

"But with golf", claimed Dash, "the reflex and instinct element is almost totally eliminated. The amount of time available preceding the swing action eliminates the reflex so vital for perfect hand and eye coordination. The design of the golf club and the turn of the shoulder, the lag component, et al, the types of gripping, wrist looseness, and swing speed and more importantly, the temperament of the player further compounded this plethora of variables and could make the game a harrowing experience for not only a learner but many a world class player. The pre-shot thought process introduces that element of doubt at the time of addressing the ball that is uppermost in every golf player's mind from the World Number One to the amateur, Dash cited the example of Darius Duvall who from being the Number 1 in the world was presently languishing at a lowly Number 180 in the world rankings within the short space of one year. Dash paused to take a large swig and continued with his story.

"The Reflex Chip", he informed, "had been developed by me to make up for the reflex and instinct element which is hugely significant when a golf swing is made. It is a silicon chip about 5 mm long and designed to be implanted in the human torso. I visualized that this invention represented the first step towards the development of the world's first cybernetic golfer or 'cyborgolfer'. Essentially, it would be surgically connected to nerve fibers in the arm; those nerves that stimulate the reflex action. The chip would also control anger and excitement (temperament), because emotions also stimulate nerve activity. I had hired the services of the famous Dr Hardwick, Professor of Cybernetics at the Southern Cross University, UK to oversee the roll out of the final product. The pioneering professor had claimed that 'it is like putting a plug into the nervous system. The overall effect I could gather is that a golfer can then compress the reflex and channelize it into the arm action for generating the swing. Another significant element of the chip was the level of club head speed it would enable the golfer to achieve; a factor so important in imparting spin and control when attacking pin positions. In addition, all chronic defects in chipping and putting would be fed into a computer and eliminated from the golfer's shots. Another innovation I introduced would be the weather data which would be fed into the chip's information system on wind speed and direction, etc. But for me, the most exciting development was the elimination of the psychological element, which in my opinion could have created havoc in Darius Duvall's game . . ."

Dash paused again to take a long swig to wet his parched throat or perhaps to blank out his misfortune. The sun had almost dipped below the horizon changing the landscape from a sea of living colors into a smudge of indeterminate grayness. A feeling of depression gripped Lang as he visualized an assembly line of mechanical golfers with no room left for the passionate amateur. He was apprehensive that this development would transform golf into just another commercial game where the element of 'glorious uncertainties' would be reduced if not eliminated altogether. He could visualize the stampede for acquiring this 'chip' by those players who were determined to improve their handicap. He gathered his thoughts together and resumed his listening.

Dash rambled on, "Earlier in the year, the research and development on the Reflex Chip was successfully concluded and I had convinced the Timber Wolf's agents to agree to the first implant. The results were indeed spectacular. The Wolf had won almost all tournaments in 2012 preceding The PGA tournament at TPC Boston which was held in late fall; and it was in the weeks leading up to this final FedEx event of the year, that the grand plan was finalized to influence the course of a tournament". Dash summarized and did not notice his friend's mournful expression.

"The Wolf", he informed," would be given directions to play consistently for the first three rounds so as to be at all times a minimum 5 strokes behind the leader. This consortium would then place bets on the victory of The Wolf with the odds stacked heavily against them. However on the last round, he would be directed to engage his 'abilities' so as to shoot an eagle on the 5th 4 Par Hole that would allow almost certainly enable him to overhaul the leader and secure victory". To ensure that Lang understand the context, Dash explained about the features of the 5th hole of the TPC Boston Golf Course,—the comparative short length measuring 377 yards and more significantly, a 280-yard narrow stretch of fairway between thick trees and dense gorse bushes, where an errant drive would almost inevitably lead to a bogey at best. He further elaborated on the gaping mouths of four hungry sand traps standing like sentinels over an undersize fast emerald like green. Dash underlined the problems and said that they further compounded by the presence of a lagoon adjoining the fairway which almost always caused a cross wind. Dash said that the score rating of the hole in the last tournament held there was a miserly 4.91 with a mere 2 percent of the field achieving birdie and whopping 70 percent carding bogies or worse, and therefore the conventional or the only approach to the pin is to hit conservatively with a mid-iron, reach the green in two and hope for a birdie.

Dash informed that in theory, the planning was perfect. The Wolf would unleash his monster drive on the 5th Hole, and reach the green in one shot. The strategy was based taking into account the reliability of the Reflex Chip implanted in The Wolf which would ensure that he would not err; an eagle on this hole would not only turn the tide in his favor but also have a psychological impact on his rivals above him on the leader board.

"Alas", Dash sighed "It was not to be. Till the 4th hole, our plan worked perfectly. After 57 holes of stroke-play, the Wolf lay 3 shots behind the leader,— who was McCarthy, the world No 1. The Wolf's odds of winning the tournament at this point in time were pegged by the bookmakers at 7 to 1. My consortium had arranged nearly half a billion dollars and had therefore borrowed heavily. All this was staked on the chances of the tournament being won by the Wolf. We distributed our bets over three continents so as not to attract unwanted attention from Interpol. Work on that final Monday (the last day of the tournament) was neglected as we sat glued to the live action on the Golf Channel.

"On the 5th Hole", Dash informed, "the Wolf as expected crunched the ball with his drive and, there was a collective gasp from the throng of spectators on seeing the audacity of the shot selection and the ball zooming onto the heart of the green. However, as it started on its path of descent, to our horror, a sparrow unexpectedly collided with the ball, and both fell into a thick gorse bush lying about 40 yards from the green. With the resultant penalty drop, it was a double bogey after that and all our substantial and borrowings went down the drain".

Dash looked at his friend expecting some sympathy, but Lang could barely conceal his elation. He was relieved that Dash's game plan had failed. The game of golf still held promise, the attraction of the unknown, the seductive 'rub of the green' for the passionate amateur, for the continuance of the 'ifs' and 'buts', dotting the conversations invariably held after every round in clubhouses around the world. And despite the best efforts of Dash and Company to make golf into a purely mechanical game devoid of the element of instinct, it would always mirror the ebb and flow, the yin and yang of everyday life. It would still provide opportunities for that 'recovery shot', for a person to utilize his skills and practice to triumph over adverse circumstances. For Lang, the game of golf was a living metaphor of honest daily effort and struggle to overcome the odds, and indeed for him this belief was an article of faith. Instead of making sympathetic noises, he raised his whisky glass in a silent toast to the gods of golf; much to the amazement of his companion who was expecting a shoulder to cry on!

TWIST IN THE TALE

I, Vishal Rai (friends know me as Vishu) never saw the golf ball until it was too late. One of those loud businessman who never heeded the honest advice of their caddies and always wanted to have the last word muffed and hooked his drive on the 13th tee box, of the Shillong Golf Course so severely that even though I had taken protective cover almost behind an old pine tree, the ball curved around the calloused trunk and hit me flush on my temple.

I woke up a fortnight later in a vile and dirty wardroom in the Civil Hospital. I later learnt that the surgeons had to remove a blood clot from my brain. Though the charges were usually nominal, some significant expenditure had been incurred for the treatment and surgery. The person responsible for my plight had outrightly refused to make any compensation claiming that it was not his fault. He claimed that he had given advance warning before hitting the ball. I was helpless to make my case especially against a prominent and influential person.

How could I pay? I did not have a penny against my name. I had been living from hand to mouth, earning a living caddying for rich and spoilt golfers who had made it in this world Well, I could have been like them. Brought up in the elite school of St Edwards, Shillong I was provided with the best education and facilities by a proud father determined to ensure that his only son would have a successful career.

He was a proud man was my father, and believed not only in a strong work ethic but also the necessity of playing sports and games. He was an officer of the Assam Regiment and encouraged me to take up golf from an early age. In this one instance, he had prevailed over my Khasi mother who normally had the last word in bringing up her son. She however made sure that my studies did not suffer. At the tender age of twelve, my handicap was already pegged at 'two' and I was competing in men's tournaments. The coaches and professional golfers saw my potential and predicted great things for me. The trophies from amateur tournaments started coming in torrents and my ability and networking opened up an opening for me as a senior marketing executive in a multi-national software corporation. However, after my father passed away soon after my mother's death from cancer, (it was known that he could not bear to live without her), I gathered the courage to leave my job and became a professional golfer.

My 265 yards 3-iron shot out of the unfriendly second rough on the notorious 17th fairway of the K.G.A. Golf Course in Bangalore saw me eagle the 5-par hole and clinch the Hero Honda Masters with its 50-lakh-rupee purse by one stroke. More handsome winnings followed and I was swinging with the rich and the famous in all those ritzy night clubs in Delhi and Mumbai. With fame came the endless partying and the accompanying fatal attractions of over friendly women and alcohol and the seductive party drugs. At that time, with money to burn, I could do no wrong. I had many 'true' friends. I was convinced that my talent and luck would see me through. Gradually, my work regimen and practice got affected and in quick succession, my discipline and resources also got depleted. With no regular job to fall back on, I became one of the boys hanging out from morning to night at the local golf club, having a bottle a day to crank up my drive or focus my putting. Any excuse was fine as long as it drove away the guilt even for an hour. Close friends avoided me as I was always on the lookout for an easy loan.

I lost my card and all my aspirations of playing on the PGA tour went up in smoke. Blaming everyone else but myself for my state of affairs, I let out my anger on everyone within sight. As a result I lost my job as a sales representative arranged by one of my uncles and to stave off penury, I was forced to become a caddy. I was good at the job but only when I was sober. I had an intimate knowledge of many a golf course and could analyze the course conditions and advise a player on the precise shot and club selection on any given day. I could even pinpoint the causes of anxiety or the apprehension of the golfer and calm his nerves.

I was to learn that one of the golfing bureaucrats, one Mr. Arvan Lang who was a member of the four—ball when I suffered my head injury had paid my medical bill and ensured that I was released from the hospital, after I had sufficiently recovered. With no house to stay in, I sought refuge in my spinster aunt's house. I had always been her favorite from early on in my life. I think my tolerance of her constant bad mood and tantrums were the reason for her hospitality. My wife whom I loved as dearly as my two children had left me when I began to self destruct, and was 'reunited' with her mother. I was to learn that she had befriended another man and was considering settling down with him I couldn't blame her. 5 years of whisky laden breath and sexual debility, is more than even the most tolerant of women could endure. Reuniting with her was out of the question. After sheltering with my aunt for almost a month, I could see that her hospitality was wearing thin.

I needed to find employment and quickly. But the job scenario was bleak. My experience as a marketing executive could not compensate for the years of my sorry life staring out from my C.V. Caddying was out of the question as my medical condition prevented me from carrying heavy weights. Further, the accident in a bizarre manner also blanked my mind from any details connected with golf. I could not distinguish between a driver and a putter. Golf tournaments even on TV sent shivers down my spine and created severe mood swings. I guess it must have been the after effects of the injury, somewhat akin to a brain stem injury which creates trauma when the victim sees things which are associated with the accident.

On the other hand, a countervailing fact that became more and more apparent after my surgery was the effect on my memory. I could memorize the entire Shillong telephone directory with a logarithm table thrown in for good measure. Believe it or not, I could read even the most technical medical text, play it back on my mind and be able to field any questions without any hesitation.

A baritone voice jerked me out of my thoughts. 'Mr. Rai?' the Big B waving a Rs. 1 crore check in his hand, asked 'Do you want to quit and go home with the Rs. I crore or proceed ahead for the final question? Yes! From being a bum shunned by all, I had achieved almost instant celebrity status. I was the first contestant from the Northeast India to make it to the penultimate round of the 2nd season of the KBC contest. I had run up sizable debts making mobile phone calls trying to log onto the KBC show. I had frequented cyber cafes logging into all the Internet sites. All those snippets, facts, records and data from historical, mythological and geographical and sporting sources I had vacuumed into my re-aligned de-clotted brain. I had surfed and scoured all important websites which specialized on giving tips and tutorials for such reality TV shows. The results were there to see. I had negotiated all the difficult questions thrown at me by the Big B. Hindu mythology, Hindi cinema, flora, fauna, cuisine, solar systems, and sports . . . (Except golf of course)

Yes! I was not dreaming. I was sitting in the Star TV Studio in Mumbai and poised to win Rs 10 crore. But, I had exhausted all my lifelines including 'phone a friend' and 50:50. I considered my options. Walk away now and win a prize which would reverse my entire fortunes and change my sorry life. Carry on but fail to answer correctly and walk away empty handed. I was literally going for broke.

And here I was, poised to turn around my sorry life with one terse alphabetic reply. I again weighed the implications. One crore rupee was mine for the taking. But I was confident of getting the other nine. I was completely cocksure about my ability to answer any damn question and I was ensconced in that false zone of certainty. I faintly registered the shouts from my cousin who had escorted me to the show and who was beseeching me to quit, to take the money and run. But with a firm nod of my head, I asked to proceed ahead.

'Are you sure', asked the Big B. in his baritone voice and I again nodded. He tore up the HSBC check for Rs 1 crore and I barely noticed the now useless bits of paper fluttering onto the floor.

THE FINAL QUESTION POSED BY THE BIG B. WAS

A NIBLICK IS A:—

    (a) A small South American rodent
    (b) A Hungarian Ice Cream
    (c) A minor injury
    (d) **A golf club!**

NORTH BY NORTHEAST

-1-

"I do not quite know why after two and a half decades of service, do I still need to attend to clerical work", Lang grumbled partly to himself as he was getting ready for work. His wife, Rita who is accustomed to his morning moods does not bother to respond and is busy giving instructions to the maid for his breakfast. Lang's mood is already spoilt after Liverpool's surprise defeat to Chelsea in their Premier League clash which has harmed their chances of winning the League. And it is further not improved by the diet restrictions imposed after his annual March medical checkup last month. Lang asks himself loudly, "No more yolk, which takes out all the character of omelet's; No butter? How does eat bread without butter, I wonder? What do you call a hamburger sans the ham?" Now he was forcing in the bland stuff and putting up a brave face. The final straw is the embargo on sugar, which means the banishment of all the good things in his life—jelabis, rasmalai, rasugulas. Then the other day Rita read on the Internet that sugar supplements were not healthy and which means that even the so called sugar free puddings and desserts have become out of bounds.

Lang is a career bureaucrat of the Indian Administrative Service (IAS) and currently posted as the Secretary to Lieutenant General (retd.) P.P. Singh, VSM,

AVSM, Governor of Meghalaya State. He also looks after the Department of Printing & Stationary, which is an additional charge. After over 20 years of less exercise and 'moderate' drinking, Lang looks older than his fifty something years. "Your paunch is here to stay", says Rita, "so you better work out on your treadmill daily", she adds. His hair has grayed and so far he has resisted all attempts to dye it black. Now his adverse cholesterol profile has encouraged his wife to finally enforce all the boring diet restrictions; Lang is now partly reconciled to being sidelined from the culinary mainstream. He also knows that he is sidelined by a bureaucratic system which he observes has morphed into a special purpose vehicle for serving political masters with no questions asked.

Lang and many of his like minded colleagues have to live with the uncomfortable reality that 'sincerity' and 'transparency', work ethics impressed upon them by their trainers in the Academy conflict directly with the people in power whose agenda is driven mainly by the arrangements with the suppliers, contractors, and crony capitalists who have become essential for ensuring re-election and creature comforts of the political masters. Lang in particular is depressed by the fact that even upright Chief Secretaries appear to be powerless against such dark forces and some of his colleagues who were known for their integrity have succumbed to the temptations of lucre and power. Lang can almost hear the tolling of the bells signaling the death knell of the service. The collapse of the steel frame is imminent, he opines to anyone who cares to listen.

On this same subject he regularly remarks to Rita. "I often wonder what is going to happen after two decades if this situation remains the same. Thank God that organized religions exist to control the silent majority, or they will not remain silent". Rita is a regular churchgoer and does not quite like his irreverent comments about religions though she tolerates he husband playing golf in all holidays and Sundays, rain, shine or religious festival. Lang feels he's been lucky in his marriage. He looks at Rita, her doe eyes and her strong chin, making up an interesting face. Despite their different religious backgrounds, and her unpredictable mood swings, they have managed over the years to identify a few common spaces where they can sort out their problems. A happy marriage is like a healthy partnership, Lang often tells his colleagues. And a plus point is that their two daughters are doing well in their higher studies.

Lang thinks that perhaps he should not be so irritated with his present posting. O.K.! In the context of his last assignment as the Secretary of the Health Department he was able to make a positive impact on the health indices of the state. The I.M.R ranking of the state had improved to a record all India 4th and had been duly appreciated by the Planning Commission. He had notified service rules for the government doctors and most of them were happy with the improvement in their service conditions. He had streamlined the supply of medical drugs to all the Government hospitals and Community medical centers and eliminated the middlemen. He was satisfied that services and hard work were now recognized and he was enthused by his contribution to efforts for uplifting the condition of the economically backward sections.

He did not regret the late nights spent in office with no regard for his health and his family obligations. The Minister was his old school friend, an honest and down to earth person. But the demand on resources for fighting the elections ensured both their exits. His Minister was made Chairman (Cabinet—Minister Rank) of a non-functional Commission on Employment Generation. Lang was looking at an obscure posting in the Secretariat but fortunately for him, a new Governor took over the office and among his first list of demands, he asked for a local IAS officer to serve as his Secretary.

Lang's duties now revolve mainly on arrangements of official functions, which involved sorting out protocol matters, attending to the Governor's wants and needs which were often interchangeable and he was frankly bored with the mundane nature of the assignment. "Arvan", his dear wife would point out. "You still have your golf to look forward to. You are getting a handsome salary and exempted from paying income tax. Stop moaning and think about your friends in other states, sometimes". Yes, Rita is almost always right, Lang conceded. He should have listened to her advice all those years ago when she told him to go easy on the pork and mutton. Now, look at him having to eat only bland and unappetizing food. He thinks about of those batch-mates who have been framed in false vigilance cases. In particular he feels sorry for a friend of the Orissa cadre who was denied promotion since 10 years and was encountering problems in even receiving his salary.

Lieutenant General P.P. Singh VSM, AVSM, accustomed to attention to the minutest detail and total obedience in his service days is yet to come to terms with the relative relaxed working style in civilian life. Though the General is known to be a good man otherwise, Lang has to bear the brunt of his list of never ending demands. Earlier in the week he summoned his Secretary. "Lang", he said condescendingly, "When I was in the Army, you know, my officers would heed my every demand and some of them could even read my mind. I remember when I needed to help a fellow 'Thakur' and transfer some tigers from one forest to another forest near his hotel. His tourist business is totally dependent on tiger sightings and all his bloody tigers had been poached or poisoned. I casually mentioned my predicament and one of my Colonels's simply requisitioned an army helicopter and flew all bloody eight big cats over a distance of 500 kilometers. Now, even my simple request for repairing the teak roof of this residence and you are talking about estimates, budgets and technical specifications. I now know why this country is in a bad shape except of course, the armed forces. You IAS people seem to be good only in file matters. Thank God, you do not have to fight a war or heaven knows, the bloody 'Pakees' would be sitting in South Block by now!"

Lang listens to all these lectures in stoic silence as he knows from previous interactions that any response would extend the monologue. The General is a physically fit man of above average height and apart from having features which are common among his genealogical stock will not stand out in a crowd. Perhaps because of this factor, he sports a bristling mustache which he twirls when he is in a bad mood. Lang and others in the bureaucracy are aware that some generals have been given gubernatorial assignments as a way of appeasing ambitious generals and not based on any outstanding merit or intellect.

That could explain why General Singh is ignorant about budget constraints, economy cuts, detailed estimates and tender committees and all those procedural requirements which are all lumped together under the definition of 'red tape'. Governors who are retired police officers are more understanding, Lang believes. They were in constant contact with the public and with politicians and are not insulated like army officers. The Governor will not listen when Lang tries to explain that Burmese teak is not available in the state and the former counters that the damn timber is readily available in Moreh on the Manipur-Myanmar border. If he was still in the army, the Governor repeats, twirling his mustache vigorously, he would have got the bloody teak brought in army trucks all the way from Manipur!

-2-

Lang has given up trying to explain official procedures and rules to the Governor. He finds solace in playing golf on the Shillong Golf Course. He also vents his woes to Sanbor Lyngdoh, his colleague, later in the weekend after the usual round of golf and over a beer in the clubhouse. He tells Sanbor, "But even more demanding is our Lady Governor. In a Republic Day function in the previous year she shouted at me in front of the staff because there were only 'four' vegetarian items in the menu—when I enquired from my oily Deputy Secretary, he informed that 'palak pakoras' she had insisted upon were not served due to a scarcity of that vegetable in Shillong. The bloody fellow should have at least given me advance warning. He must have done it on purpose to make me lose face. I know that he is trying to get me shunted out after I vetoed his plan to appoint a close relative as a cook. Listen, there was another incident. Madam got further incensed when the Assam muga silk curtains she ordered to be installed in every window could not be immediately complied with as sanction was needed for the expenditure. The building is of the Tudor style and there are more windows than you can count. And now her bloody husband is also eating up my head!"

Sanbor is in a reflective mood drinking his beer allowing Lang to carry on with his tirade. The latter continues, "What really gets my goat is the amount of time and application of mind on protocol matters—who is to sit where and with the warrant of precedence at odds with the importance and power of the office, it is indeed a Sisyphean task to satisfy and prevent heartburns. I am told that in some earlier function the respective ADCs of the Air Force Marshal and the Army General both posted in Shillong had almost come to blows in trying to force primacy of position for their bosses. In another function held at the Darbar Hall I was publicly admonished when the Director General of Police was given a seat in front of the Principal Secretary, Political Department next to the Chief Secretary of the State. Last month, there was another high drama over the seating arrangements for a dinner organized in honor of the Dalai Lama and you should have seen Lady Governor's . . ." Sanbor's mind is somewhere else by now and his friend's voice does not register.

Sanbor and Lang trained together in the IAS Academy in Mussoorie and though they still meet frequently because of their golfing weekends, the former has been having problems with his marriage and has socially drifted away. Lang used to admire Sanbor—his open and expressive face, love of all outdoor activities; his quick wit and strong repartee. As he looks at his colleague friend he now sees a man whose eyes are pools of disquiet, suspicious of stray comments and ready to pick up quarrels for imagined slights. Lang is vaguely aware of Sanbor's marital problems but does not want to pry.

Sanbor in fact is actually having problems in his marriage. At the moment he is remembering his turbulent courtship days. Daphisha, his wife was so vivacious then. She was so attractive that friends and family and indeed the people who knew were surprised when she chose poor Sanbor over other suitors. 'Must have been the IAS brand', Sanbor thinks. He vaguely remembers the other contenders—the rich businessman with the Maruti car dealership, the PWD engineer with the fancy foreign car and who he learnt had proposed with a 25 lakh rupee diamond ring. But she had been drawn to him for he had recognized her aspirations, her need to spread her wings that were still furled by the restrictions imposed by her conservative Presbyterian upbringing and the strictness of her parents. During their courtship which was strongly discouraged by her family, he discovered aspects of her character—her sense of adventure, her thirst for travel and her dream of doing social work. He was confident that through true love, her potential would be realized and the barriers she erected around herself would be broken down.

Was he wrong? Maybe, Daphisha married him because he had cleared the exams for the prestigious Indian Administrative Service. For over the years the lights in their rooms went out one after another. Or maybe, he did not live up to her materialistic expectations or she was influenced by gossip and insinuation about his past life. She slowly retreated into a zone of silence which for him became a no go area. He was relieved by the fact that his two children, a boy and a girl were pursuing studies outside Shillong. Sanbor would often think that because of Daphisha's sense of insecurity she was reverting again to those familiar practices in her childhood, her church services, her Bible reading; activities which he always maintained were a waste a time.

Thus, the barriers between them were becoming more insurmountable by the day. And her crazy mood swings! He had never shared Lang's view that a happy marriage was like a successful partnership. He long held the view that true love was the sole driving force which would permanently sustain even the most turbulent of relationships. Now he was coming to realize that Lang's point was not wrong after all. He remembered Dylan's lines, 'True love tends to forget' which given the situation he was in had now become so relevant. He had often thought about consulting a marriage counselor or even a psychiatrist? He has tried his best—making a nice house, trying to attend to her every need . . . He has given so much for his children and the only time he is happy is when he reflects on their progress. Now, on their own he endures the long sullen silences and has learnt to insulate himself from the constant retorts.

Sanbor has personally experienced the pain of parental indifference. He was the fourth among seven offspring and had been brought up by parents who wielded the cane even for the most minor transgression. He and the other siblings came to acknowledge that their parents brought them up in a way where communication and bonding with the children was something foreign to their culture. He was determined that his children would not lack for love and attention. Nevertheless, he had contemplated divorce and even consulted a lawyer. He came to dread those long lonely nights where he would often think about divorce. He would feel for his children and the trauma of separation. But he can now barely tolerate the strain of being trapped in a failed marriage. No sex for as long as he can remember. Watching porn and self gratification does not compensate or satisfy, feels Sanbor. Then along comes Tamara who provided an exciting alternative option. She is about thirty years old, a divorcee and working as a policy analyst in one of the government departments.

He nods his head up and down seemingly in agreement with Arvan's arguments but his mind still does not register. His thoughts are churning on the pros and cons of a long term affair with Tamara. He had noticed her figure, the tight blue jeans and the low cut red top, when she crossed him on the corridor of the Main Secretariat. What made her stand out was her outfit which were not the traditional 'jain-sems' worn by the female employees of the government. He found out that she worked in one of the sections in the Finance Department and he would often pass by her room to sneak a look.

Those sorties must have been detected. She gave him the 'eye' in some meeting he attended in the Secretariat Conference Hall and her deliberate touch when she handed him the agenda papers sent a bolt of electricity through his very being. He had needed to obtain a different mobile number and buy another new mobile phone to avoid suspicion. Thereafter, a series of SMS and Whatsapp interactions had eventually led to a series of furtive couplings on the hard and narrow sofa in his office room in the last three months.

"What a filly"! Sanbor ruminates. Tamara is attractive with an oval face and a pert nose, features which are characteristically Khasi, though she is above average in height and whitish in complexion. He is thinking about her tight body, mango shaped breasts, and her ruby red lips and contrasts these assets with the poutiness and dowdiness of his wife. More than that, he feels that he is falling in love. Tamara has a way of arching her left eyebrow and puckering her lips slightly which drives him to distraction whenever he is with her. And she is so bubbly and interactive in their phone conversations. Sanbor sometimes though senses an undertone of insecurity and mental frailty in her character. But at least he is not lonely anymore.

Sanbor is aware that that he will enter unknown waters if Tamara consents to his plan. He weighs the cost. He realizes that his world will soon entail telling white lies, half truths, staying late in the office, excuses for work load. Apart from these issues, there lies the possibility of getting discovered and the inevitable social consequences. He pushes all these problems to the back of his mind, and thinks about the additional expenditure required for his foray. He figures that he needs to generate an extra monthly income of about Rupees 40 thousand to be able to sustain the affair which will include renting an apartment and other contingencies. He therefore would need to dip into his savings, and withdraw from his GPF fund and open an online trading account—Dr. Reddy, ICICI Bank, Bio-Tech maybe? He has noted that their shares are consistently yielding handsome returns despite the frequent ups and downs of the SENSEX. Probably to justify his infidelity, Sanbor tells Lang who has concluded his complaints, "One can never know what is going to happen tomorrow; see what happened to Aibok (one of their golfing friends who lost his life in a car accident)—the good indeed die young!

-3-

Lang is happy that he has his golfing and the bonhomie and repartee to turn to during the postmortems after the rounds. Discussions get heated when they analyze the merits and skill of their 'recovery shots'. In particular, chilled Budweiser beer tastes like ambrosia after 18 holes. And taking his handicap of 16 into consideration, he had played reasonably well shooting a twelve over par. Plus, he and Sanbor had won the game raking in winnings which covered their caddy fee and the beer.

But, Lang has to get a move on. His driver has brought his official Hyundai Verna car to the front of the house. Today is April the 13th, a Saturday, the day scheduled for the swearing in of the new Cabinet. The Chief Minister, the wily Hekson Momin, is set to retain his leadership as he has the backing of the High Command and the blessings of 'Madam'. The Congress Party has secured a simple majority in the 60 member Assembly but the general feeling amongst the majority of the public is one of 'angst'. There is no sense of anticipation which is normally associated when a new Government is about to take over. For, it is well known that with the threat of revolt always hanging over Momin's head, it will take a Herculean effort on his part to ensure his own survival and at the same time bring about improvement in the development of

Meghalaya where almost all program funds sanctioned by the Government of India are diverted for other non-development activities.

Lang can imagine the mood and thoughts of those other twenty overlooked M.L.A.s. conspiring and plotting strategies for securing precious ministerial berths. Can you blame them, thinks Lang. They need to recover all the investments and repay all the debts they have incurred for winning their elections. The indelible ink on his finger is barely dry and Lang feels sorry for Mr. Momin who instead of focusing on generating employment opportunities and sustainable development for the state is surely planning on ways and means for generating adequate resources for tightening his grip. He is surely thinking about the portfolios he has to keep to himself. He must be thinking about those officers who will rally to his cause. This leads to a job environment where some officers will bend procedures to achieve short term gains for their Ministers, rues Lang. He had earlier worked with Nekson who was then a Minister in charge of the Rural Development Department. Lang had objected to a supply order and was eased out. He knows from this experience, that the Chief Minister hides his vindictive nature behind an easy smile and a permanently outstretched hand.

Lang commutes the short distance from his residential quarter to his office. The route runs along the Ward's Lake which has not dried up due to the water being replenished by an underground spring. In 1897, the lake burst its banks but after repair of the check dam, it filled up within weeks. He thinks of the drying Umiam Lake and the insufficient power being generated. Dark days lie ahead, indeed, says Lang loudly to himself as he acknowledges the sentry's salute at the gate to the Governor's residence. Lang's office is located within the grounds of the Governor's House and on the left side of the main building. He takes two minutes to reach the Governor's office walking through the rose garden. It is ironical, thinks Lang. The whole town is reeling from sever water shortages due to a prolonged drought and here the sprinklers are used extensively for watering the flower gardens and the expansive lawns.

He mentally goes over the arrangements for the function. He has readied all the twelve files which need to be signed by the incoming Chief Minister and his other twelve M.L.A.s He instructs his Deputy Secretary to make sure that the tea and snacks are to be made ready by 1300 hours and served in the new hall which also doubles up as a badminton court. The Governor and the Chief Minister will however take their tea in the library away from the madding crowd. He strides up the steps leading up to the main door and into the foyer with the miniature brass cannon on the left. Directly ahead is another door with the inscription on a plaque above it. It reads, 'My uncle is not greater than my country', which were the words uttered by the Ahom King, Lachit Borphukan when he beheaded his traitorous uncle during the Ahom-Mughal Wars. Ironic in these modern times! says Lang aloud. Turning left, he walks alongside portraits of Naga warriors, pastoral scenery, spears, shields, swords and other implements of war exhibited on the wooden walls. He then enters the office of the Governor and verbally submits his action taken report for the function. General Singh seems satisfied with the preparations and dismisses Lang who then returns to his office.

Today is a holiday and Lang should be on the course playing golf instead of fussing over trivial matters. His mother once chided him on his playing golf on holidays instead of devoting some more time to his family. Lang who often never replies back because she is very old and easily irritated, for once felt the need to respond. And he knows that Rita must have complained to her. He had said, "Mei, we play for fun and for small stakes. And golf is an outlet for our frustration with the system and it provides some physical activity. Then there is the added attraction of the 'nineteenth hole' where we can play cards and banter without the close attention of our better halves. Of course, I cannot do without my wife and she has given so much for my sake. But, sometimes, don't we men need to be by ourselves?" His mother had simply shaken her head but she has not bothered him lately about his golf and gambling.

That dialogue happened some years ago, Lang recalls, reflecting with some degree of satisfaction that his marriage is healthy notwithstanding the ups and downs; like a normal ECG reading he muses. He is fortunate that he is not having problems like Sanbor. He looks around the office and notices that one of the planks of the wooden floor need to be replaced. He also makes a mental note to instruct the PWD to renovate the electrical wiring and to install the modern MCB cut-off system. The room has not changed since it was rebuilt after the 1897 earthquake. His office table is made of solid 'gamari' wood and its top is fitted with a thick green billiard like felt cloth. The original chair though has been exchanged for a modern ergonomic Godrej chair on account of his cervical problem. The glass cabinets and the cupboards are all made of

Burmese teak and their dark polish reflects the solid exposed rafters on the high ceiling. Over the years, the collection of rare books purchased by the office has increased in number and is prominently displayed in the old cabinets. It has been unusually hot by Shillong standards but the oversize windows and the cross ventilation of the room obviates the need for an air conditioner. This office chamber is one consolation in his present assignment, he realizes as it makes up for the stuffiness and stifling heat in former office in the Main Secretariat.

-4-

It is almost 1 p.m. and he calls for the peon to take the files to the Durbar Hall where the swearing in ceremony will be held. The Governor had agreed to the suggestion made by the Chief Minister to begin the program at 1.13 P.M. Obviously, this time must have been chosen by some astrologer as being auspicious. Politicians will embrace any measure, even if they are irrational just to give them confidence, thinks Lang. He enters the Durbar Hall and makes sure that the chairs are positioned in their correct places on the podium. He checks the security arrangements and the readiness of the police band that will play the national anthem before and after the function. It so happened that a couple of years earlier, the band could not perform due to the drunken condition of the band members playing the tuba and the trombone! A tape recorder was frantically arranged but the tinny sound of the national anthem was barely audible much to the embarrassment of the Governor's Secretary!

The ceremony starts at the scheduled time and it is stifling inside the Darbar Hall. It is unusually hot by Shillong standards with the mercury touching almost thirty degrees Celsius. The swearing in process is about to get over and as expected, those M.L.A.s who have been overlooked can barely conceal their resentment. If minds could be read, you would guess correctly that Nelson Lyngdoh, the prominent coal baron who has been elected from Nartiang Constituency after splurging over Rs 800 million is already calculating the money needed to stage a coup d'état. It will not matter to him if more coal mines are exploited and more limestone is mined. If will not matter to these democratically elected leaders if more forests are plundered and more rivers are polluted. Lang looks around and sees another M.L.A. from the Garo Hills who is a surrendered extremist. Lang cannot remember his full name . . . something Sangma, but he was told that this former rebel has several cases of murder and extortion pending against him.

Another M.L.A, Mrs Alka Kharbam is amongst the last to be sworn in. She represents an urban constituency. She has been recently implicated in a major agriculture scam and it is common knowledge that she won her elections through purchase of votes from the very poor sections of her constituency. He sees another M.L.A., Ban Mador who began his political career as a firebrand student leader and won elections through stoking of communal passions. Now, he is a multi millionaire with houses in Bangalore and Delhi. Most of the bureaucrats openly voice the opinion that the Model Code of Conduct imposed by the Election Commission of India is just cosmetic in nature. 'Where is the rule of law?' asks Lang silently. Here are our leaders swearing in the name of God and loyalty to our Constitution? Statehood even after forty years is yet to bring sustainable improvement in our lives, thinks Lang

Almost all present are freely perspiring and are looking forward to making their escape to the cooler environment of the badminton hall where the tea and snacks will be served. Many of his colleagues are also present. Attendance in these functions is compulsory by Government order. Some of the senior officers wear expressions of faithful attentiveness. One of them in particular is very close to the C.M. His name is K.L. Sinha and he is from one of the states in mainland India. He is a couple of years junior to Lang in service but he has the C.M.'s confidence and has been entrusted with almost all the important departments. Sinha is known for his expertise in anticipating the wishes of his political masters and facilitating their agenda. Apart from this expertise, he is also a past master in covering not only his own tracks but that of his political bosses. The bureaucracy knows that replacing the man will be a difficult task for the C.M. as Sinha will be proceeding on deputation to New Delhi. Lang and many others were hoping that the C.M.'s re-election would herald a positive phase for the state. But going by the selection of Ministers, and allocation of portfolios, it seems that status quo will be retained. Lang sighs at the futility of it all.

Lang sees the Deputy Secretary sidling up to him who whispers that his office has caught fire! Oh God! Lang's first thought is of the century plus old office building and records and files which will surely be destroyed. He somehow manages to exit the hall without being noticed though the smell of the smoke has now become apparent to everyone inside. The sound of the sirens of the fire tenders has also become fully audible to everyone in the Hall. By the time Lang reaches his office, the Tudor style building has almost burnt to the ground. The prolonged drought and the unrelenting heat aided by a brisk spring breeze have all contributed to the inferno. Nothing can be salvaged. All the computers and gadgets have melted. Lang looks at the razed area where the two guest rooms were located. The kitchen and the dining room are totally gutted. Lang agonizes over the loss of the rare books, the original journals written by former Chief Commissioners of Assam, the diaries of the legendary District Magistrates. He shakes his head sadly when he thinks of all those photographs, films and his incomplete novel which he had meant to store on Google Drive.

Ten days later and Lang has relocated to a stuffy room in the Secretariat Building. An official inquiry has been initiated to find out the cause of the fire though he is certain that the electrical wiring was to blame. Some rumors have started circulating though and which are being encouraged by reporters of some of the papers. The other day, he was confronted by Billy Roy, an aggressive reporter from the Shillong Tribune who had asked whether the fire was due to arson as he, Billy, had learnt from 'reliable' sources that a file relating to an inquiry on a land acquisition case was being put up to the Governor for authorizing a CBI inquiry? Now, was it a fact that all the records were in that file? Lang makes a 'no comment' reply and the next day, the front page of the paper reports that a case of arson has not been ruled out.

Lang mentally readies himself for the flood of queries through the RTI gateway which will increase his workload and he hopes that at least his golf is not too badly affected. He reflects that after the advent of the RTI Act, the job of the IAS officer has become more complicated. Damned if you do, and damned if you don't, thinks Lang aloud. And the bloody number of meetings! It has gotten worse after P.C. Shukla, returned from Delhi after a five year deputation with the Planning Commission and given the charge of the Planning & Development Department. Meetings have become longer and more boring with lengthy power point presentations expounding ambitious and unviable programs and schemes.

-5-

It is 1500 hrs and his mobile phone beeps. It is the ADC to the Governor who informs him that the boss would like to see him, immediately! General Singh would like to discuss the reconstruction of the burnt office. Lang eventually exits from the main entrance of the Secretariat Building glancing up at the giant clock which overlooks the car park and the statue of Gandhi. It's already past 1530 hours and the Governor will not be happy at having to wait. The distance from the Secretariat Building to the Governor's House is not even a kilometer but because of traffic snarls, it can take even up to 10 minutes. His driver weaves through the traffic trying to avoid the jams. The car rounds the Deputy Commissioner's office and passes in front of the office of the Accountant General with the picturesque Ward's Lake to the left.

Though he is running behind time, Lang gets down at the entrance gate of the Governor's House and sends his car ahead. There were heavy showers throughout the night bringing much needed relief from the heat and the dust and he wants to walk through the grounds. Till yesterday, the leaves and needles of the old pine trees and the conifers lining the driveway were dirty brown and bone dry. Now they have turned sparkling green and the lawns look refreshed. The aroma emanating from a combination of wet pine needles and moist loamy earth is refreshing. A gentle breeze wafts through and around the cluster of trees and ruffles the azaleas. He breathes in the air and forgets about his hassles. He hears a cuckoo nearby and tries to locate it but it is too elusive. A woodpecker is busy at work in the woods at the bottom of the garden located left of the building. Some of the fruit trees next to the musical fountain have flowered and the pink blossoms of the peach tree counterpointed by the white flowers of the pear trees and framed by the rolling lawns are reminiscent of a scene from one of Keats's poems. Overhead, he sees dozens of swifts circling and wheeling against the azure blue sky.

Luckily, the remnants of his office are hidden by the thick hedge on the right of the main building. He sees that around the perimeter of what was once an office, the grass is singed and the flower beds have all been trampled by the firemen. Lang tries to form a mental picture of the new building though he knows that reconstruction in the original Tudor style is out of the question. He mentally tries to anticipate what the Governor would want. He would probably say, "I want a replica of the original building. If needed, source the material from England, I would manage the reconstruction myself if I was still in the Army . . ."

Lang smiles to himself at the thought and is about to cross over through the garden to meet the boss when he notices a blackened object resembling part of an iron box protruding out of the ground. The spot, Lang remembers is approximately the same where the dislodged plank was located on his office floor. It could have been a trapdoor to a hiding place below the floor, Lang feels. He thinks that the box could have been overlooked when it was covered by soot and mud and which had since been washed away by the overnight rain.

With minimum effort, Dan his driver pulls out the box which is not too heavy. He estimates its measurements to be around 14 inches in length, 8 inches in width and about ten inches in depth. Lang instructs Dan to place the box in the boot of his car. He then enters the office chamber of the Governor who does not hide his displeasure of having to wait. Lang can barely contain his anticipation at the thought of opening the old metal box and hardly pays attention to the discussion. As expected the Governor wants estimates to be framed 'immediately' by the PWD and he wants the building to house both office and residence! Lang excuses himself and returns to his office. But he does not want to take the iron box to his office in front of curious eyes and wagging tongues. He will inventory the contents if they are of some value and file a report to his Chief Secretary, if need be.

-6-

Lang can barely conceal his disappointment. He is sitting in a room in his house which doubles up as a study. With the help of a screwdriver, the cover of the box has been removed. The contents of the box appear to be a manuscript of some sort. Some pages have been half burnt and still some others besides the file cover have been slightly singed by the fire. He gingerly takes out the manuscript carefully and unties the thread holding the file together careful not to let the pages shred and fall. Lang can barely make out the title on the partially burnt file cover but he thinks it reads as

'MY . . . . ASSAM (1913-1947)'
BY JAMES P. MILLS (ICS)

Lang remembers from reading about the history of the region that Mills was the Secretary to the Governors of Assam from 1930, the last being Sir Andrew Clow, 1945 to 1947. He had also read somewhere that Mills through his experiences in the Naga Hills had authored two monographs, *The Ao Nagas* in 1926 and earlier to this, *The Lotha Nagas* in 1922. He had then taken up a position in the faculty of the School of Oriental and African Studies in London after his retirement from the ICS in 1947. He held the same position as was held presently by Lang and he must have worked in the same office room. That would explain why the manuscript was kept in the box and concealed in the hiding place. But he cannot understand why Mills forgot about his journal. Perhaps in the tumultuous days after India achieved its independence the British were in a hurry to evacuate and forgot about the hiding place. Lang makes up his mind to report and return the find to the Government. But first, he has decided to read the journal. Apart from Rita and Dan, he is sure that no one knows yet about the mysterious metal box. Anyway, the contents appear to be of little value Lang thinks and once reported to Government and returned he is sure that the file would be kept in some corner and forgotten.

Lang forgoes his round of golf in the weekend much to the surprise of Sanbor and the other two friends of his regular four-ball. He has made up his mind to attempt to read the partly charred manuscript and he wants to devote a full Saturday for the task. Rita is equally surprised for she has been echoing his mother's sentiments about his neglect of his family for the sake of his beloved golf. Lang retreats to his study with a mug of La-kyrsiew green tea, opens the file cover and begins to read the first page.

I was born in 1890 in Yaoundé in the British part of Cameroon and my family shifted to England when I was about 2 years of age due to my mother's ill health. My father was a coffee planter but from an early age my imagination was fired up by tales of Africa and India and I wanted to work in the 'Empire'. I graduated from Corpus Christi College in 1913 and qualified later in the same year for

the Indian Civil Service. After almost one year of
training and orientation, I departed for India on
29th April, 1914 from the Liverpool docks on the S.S.
Providence. The memory of the R.M.S. Titanic was
still fresh in everyone's mind as my family crowded
around me for my farewell.

As I was about to board, a headline on the Daily
Mail caught my attention. 'Archduke Ferdinand and
his wife Sophie assassinated in Sarajevo'! Though
the paper did not mention about any reaction from
the Emperor of Austro-Hungary and his allies, my
insights and perceptions of the political situation
in Central Europe warned me that a major conflict
was imminent. Would Great Britain be involved if
a war arose between Austro-Hungary, Germany on
one side and my country and Russia on the other?
Would my services be required in that case? These
silent doubts were forgotten as the ship was towed
out by tugs and the waving of goodbyes to the crowds
on the quay. Once the city slipped out of sight a drill
was held where we were assigned lifeboat stations
and tables for our meals. Thereafter we checked out
our cabins and I found out that my fellow occupant,
a Mr. Andrew Pierce was also headed for India to
take up an assignment in a tea garden in the Jorhat
district of Assam. This was a coincidence because
my first posting was to be as a sub-division officer at
Mokokchung, subdivision in the Naga Hills District
which was not too far from Jorhat.

Contrary to my apprehension, the voyage was not
all that boring. Several deck games were organized
such as shuffle board and deck tennis and in fact
there was even an area for a golf practice range which

was cordoned by a thick net. A couple of niblicks and fairway woods and about two dozen used Dunlop balls could be hired and I passed quite a bit of time on the voyage whacking balls onto a tarpaulin. When I had to quit golf about a year ago to focus on my preparations for the ICS exam, I was playing to a respectable handicap of 14. Through casual inquiries with old India hands on the availability of golf courses in Northeast India, I was informed that there was a golf course in the town of Shillong.

I had to dress formally for dinner as I was invariably invited to dine at the captain's table. Meals were elaborate and some of the dishes had exotic flavors and the preparations were definitely superior to many of the restaurants in London. To this day, I can still recall the taste of the roast lamb and rosemary and the gooseberry layer shortcake. I was informed by the captain that many of the chefs were influenced by foreign cuisines in their travels on the seven seas. After dinner, we would retire to the captain's study for cognac and cigars. Though I was not much of a drinker, I would accompany Pierce to the bar where he would absorb prodigious quantities of Scotch without being much the worse for wear. In fact, I was often the victim having to tolerate his loud snoring throughout the nights.

We sailed south across the Bay of Biscay which surprisingly was calm and onto the Mediterranean Sea. Our first stop was at the Port Said the entrance to the Suez Canal. Pierce and I went ashore and were immediately surrounded by peddlers selling all sorts of wares. One of the attractions was a native who enthralled the passengers with magic tricks such *as taking out white pigeons from their ears. Back on board and the ship along with the rest of the convoy entered the canal the progress determined by a speed limit as exceeding of the same would create a wake strong enough to damage the sides of the canal.*

We left Suez behind and after some hours, the ship moored to a buoy at Aden and we were transported by a launch to the port. The old town of Aden was situated right in the middle of an ancient crater and in fact, one could only enter the settlement through a gap in the crater wall. We were mildly surprised when we were told that Aden was administered as a part of British India and known as the Aden Settlement. I thought to myself that there was a possibility that I could one day be posted to this place and I quite liked the prospect as I had a fondness not only for anthropology but for archeology also.

After spending a night at the Crescent Hotel we were taken back to the ship and onto our final destination of Bombay. The time taken for the final leg we were told would be over 36 hours and midway, we were hit by the beginning of the Southeast monsoon. Though the ship was really yawing and rolling, I comforted myself with the thought that my ancestors of the East India Company braved such weather in fragile wooden ships. Pierce however became quite seasick and for once forgot about his nightly comfort of 'Dewar's' White Label!

The next day was not much better and as the ship approached Bombay the Gateway of India loomed suddenly out of the sea fog. We were taken ashore and where I was told that I would be put up at the

Taj Hotel, regarded as the best hotel in the city next only to Watson's Hotel. I was quite intrigued by Taj Hotel. Though imposing in structure and singular by way of its Indo-Saracen style of architecture, its back was to the sea and to the Gateway of India. I was told that this was deliberately designed as the other side provided easier access for guests travelling on their horse carriages. I was now alone as I was given to understand that Pierce had been lodged in another hotel by his employers—McNeill and McGregor Tea Pvt. Ltd. Despite the high ceilings of the room and the enormous ceiling fans, I could not quite sleep due to the humidity and the close confines of the bed net. I anticipated that the climate of the entire country was something similar and the faster I got used to it, the better. I was also feeling lonely in an alien environment and missing the hearty company of Mr. Pierce, but again the quicker I got used to my living conditions, the better.

The next morning, I was taken by a horse drawn carriage to the Victoria Terminus, a bustling rail station in the middle of the city and not very far from the hotel to board the Imperial Indian Mail bound for Calcutta. I was told that the entire journey would take more than 36 hours and I would probably be able to reach my place of posting after a week. I was quite depressed thinking about the remoteness of my posting and equally distraught that despite my impressive academic record at Corpus Christi College, Oxford and after many months of intensive preparation, I could not quite make the cut for the 'Home Service' or even the 'Diplomatic Service', but instead qualified for the ICS. I learnt that out of the maximum marks of 1900 I needed 1300 or more to qualify for the 'Diplomatic' and 1500 or more for the 'Home' Service. But I must admit that I quite enjoyed the orientation course I attended at the Institute for Oriental and African Studies, London where we had to learn the Hindi and Bengali languages and the finer points of law and public administration.

The station platforms were very crowded except for those areas which gave access to the 'whites only' compartments. They resembled the vortex in a tornado with frenetic activity all around but eerily still at the center. I boarded a 1st class compartment, feeling sorry for the mass of humanity crammed into the unreserved and 3rd class compartments. I was the lone passenger in my compartment and looking at my immediate surroundings came to the conclusion that I would do quite well till I arrived at my destination. There were twin berths, with the upper one being folded upwards when not in use during the day. A chain with the notice, 'Pull to stop the train. Wrong use will attract a fine of One Rupee only' hung above and between two windows each which had three types of covering—one with fine netting, the second made of glass and the third with stout bars. I was also fortunate to have an attached bathroom with a cast iron washbasin and a water shower. During the long journey, I did not have to venture out for meals as orders were taken by waiters attired in livery and wearing tall turbans. I later learnt that my orders were wired to the next station and the meals were made ready by the time the train arrived . . .

-7-

'**O**h shit'! Lang sees that he cannot proceed further as very many pages are partially charred and the words have become illegible. He imagines Mr. Mills wending his way over the vast flat countryside from Bombay to Calcutta in 1914. Not much had changed by way of rail transport, thought Lang. At present, it would still take almost a week to reach Kohima from Bombay by train and road. And Mills was correct in predicting the advent of the Great War which commenced exactly one month after the assassination of the Archduke Ferdinand. He gingerly peels off the burnt pages till the next intact portion and it is evident that the major portion of the manuscript has been totally damaged. He ignores his wife's call for lunch and continues with his reading . . .

. . . indeed how time has flown! Over 30 years ago I arrived in this country and I can vividly remember my departure from Liverpool and the voyage to Bombay. I landed on these shores just before the start of the Great War and now I am about to leave this country which has been my home for thirty plus years soon after the end of World War II. I will not recount my experiences in the Naga Hills as my two monographs have dwelled at length on these subjects. I get depressed when I think of the relatives and friends who went missing during the two Great Wars.

I often wonder also what happened to Pierce. We lost touch after we went our separate ways. I later learnt from an ICS colleague that he was posted as an Assistant Manager in Halem Tea Estate near Tezpur. This town was quite distant from my place of posting and my attempts to establish contact came to naught.

Suffice it to say that after spending almost a couple of decades in the Naga Hills, I have occupied this post of Secretary to Governor now for close to 15 years. The murmurs for an independent India have now grown into loud rumblings and even more ominous is the demand for a separate homeland for the Muslims. I fear for the future of the tribes of this region. Without the protection and rights guaranteed by us, they will be swamped and their land gobbled up by the people from the plains. In fact, I had sought to address this problem by writing a note on the future of Hill Tribes of Assam. In short, I had suggested that all the hill tribes of the region including those in Burma should be placed under the direct administrative control of the Governor of Assam. Tribal councils could be constituted either through direct elections or nomination and they could be delegated certain financial and judicial powers. Further, they could also be authorized to nominate one representative in the Governor's Council.

However, I have recommended that the Khasi Tribe should be left out of the above dispensation. I have interacted with their leaders from time to time and I have come to the conclusion that they have been influenced to a large extent by us. They can hold their own in any meeting with their counterparts from the plains. Perhaps due the presence of a judicial system in Shillong, they are very litigant and tend to seek relief from the courts rather than settle matters amongst themselves. The majority of them has also converted to Christianity and appears to have lost their distinctive tribal culture. They therefore will be able to fend for themselves in any situation. The Governor, Sir Andrew Clow had kindly informed me that he had forwarded my note to the Governor General, Lord Wavell and to Mr. L.S. Amery, the Secretary of State for India . . .

Lang shakes his head not only because of the illegible words which follows but also of this misconception of Mr. Mills. No doubt, he thinks to himself, his tribe has been influenced to a great deal by the colonialists, and many amongst the Khasis including his wife have converted to Christianity. But even at present, the majority of them still follow the 'Niam Trai' religion which is based on the recognition of one God, he feels. Lang thinks of the social convention, 'Tip Briew, Tip Blei' (Constant awareness of God through respect for all humans), 'Im Lang, Sah Lang' (Unity through togetherness), 'Ka Ktien kaba Tam' (the primary value of the word). All of these and many more conventions and practices formed the basis for a culture and an identity which evolved over time and are still observed and recognized as a means of a reunion with the Creator in the afterlife. 'True', reflects Lang. 'We do not have the more visible symbols of tribalism— the hand-woven shawls and the elaborately designed sarongs, the system of chieftainship, the rice beers and exotic food, but for the Khasis, the identity and his mindset are what stills set him apart from the people on the mainland. We have an elaborate code of etiquette which is still adhered to and has won the admiration of many a European including Major P.T. Gurdon. More importantly, the primacy of the clan and the observance of the social convention of 'khein kur, khein kha' where related clans cannot intermarry is one of the distinguishing hallmarks of the tribe and an effective genetic weapon against the menace of inbreeding which has decimated many small communities. Even the converted ones, be it Catholic or Protestant are still adhering to these customs. Further he had read in Wikipedia that the Khasis closely resembled the Cherokee tribe of North America in their matrilineal practices. If this was not a distinctive culture. Lang asks himself, then what is?

After a hurried and cold lunch, he resumes his reading of the partially burnt manuscript . . .

Today, the 6th January, 1947 I was summoned by the Governor and he informed that an agreement had been reached between Mountbatten the new Viceroy of India, the Indian National Congress and Jinnah to partition India on religious lines. I was also informed that one Mr. Cyril Radcliffe had been appointed by His Majesty to finalize the process. Sir Clow however told me in strict confidentiality that the Viceroy would take the final decision as Radcliffe had been selected only for his legal expertise and not for his knowledge of the country and its demographics. For that reason alone, Mountbatten needed advice and suggestions from those Governors who were connected with the provinces to be affected, viz. Punjab, Bengal and Assam. This feedback was immediately needed as the Prime Minister Sir Clement Atlee wanted to hand over the country within the next six months. It is evident that post war Britain in deep debt and recession could not maintain an empire for much longer. My heart bleeds for my beloved country and for is rapid slide since I last left its shores.

Lang is quite surprised at what he has just learnt. It was common knowledge that Radcliffe had been heavily criticized for the bloodbath and ethnic cleansing which was caused by his actions. It was widely reported that he had destroyed all papers and records connected with the Partition process before he left India. Historians were of the unanimous view that he had been specially appointed by Clement Atlee to partition the country because of his ignorance of the ground conditions and with his legal mind could finish his job quickly. It was reported that he reported to nobody and his decisions were totally independent. The four member commission set up to assist him did not have any expertise in land surveys and were almost useless. This appeared to be the case as he had apparently drawn lines dividing even residential houses in some areas of Bengal and Punjab. But, if what Mills had written was indeed factual, Radcliffe must have reported to Lord Mountbatten and under instructions drawn his controversial lines. In that case, the records would have to be set right for that era. But, this would again depend on the evidence left behind by J.P. Mills in the burnt journal. What a find it would be! With mounting excitement, Lang reads on . . .

Today, the 2ndst May 1947, my recommendations for the Partition of Assam are almost finalized. I have suggested that the districts of Sylhet and Mymensingh should be included with the new

Dominion of Pakistan. Though many districts of lower Assam are dominated by Muslims, overall the majority of the population is Hindu. In this respect, as I had indicated in my earlier note, the hill tribes of the Northeast need some special protection and for this reason, their areas may be included in India. This arrangement will also cover the tribes of the Chittagong Hills. They will be ensured better treatment than by the Muslims. In this regard, special tribal councils for them can be created to be made accountable to the Governor of Assam. In this way, they will be self administered and insulated from the administrative control of the Chief Minister of the Province. Alternatively, dominion status maybe considered for them as a special case on account of their distinctive identity and culture though this will constitute an extreme measure . . .

However, I have reiterated what I had written in my aforesaid note on the 'excluded areas' that the Khasis can look after themselves as they have lost almost all their tribal culture, and as the new dominion of East Bengal will require at least one hill station, the Khasi and Jaintia Hills maybe included in the district of Sylhet. In addition, I have also received representations from some of the Khasi chiefs who own large plantations in the Sylhet area. I am of the opinion that they feel that they will be better off in East Bengal so that they do not lose their assets. I have also recommended that the Garo Hills should be tagged along as the majority of the tribe resides in Sylhet and Mymensingh District. Shillong is located in almost exactly north of Sylhet and within Northeast India. Therefore communication links between the two towns will not pose a problem in future. Further, in this regard, Sir Andrew received a letter from Mohammed Ali Jinnah which was handed over to me forwarding a representation from a Mr. R. Ahsan of the Calcutta District Muslim League who has written that, 'the loss of Calcutta and Assam is terrible . . . if we get the excluded areas of Parganas, Khasi and Jaintia Hills, . . . we will get room for expansion'.

-8-

L ang ponders over what would have been the present
situation if his beloved Shillong and the emerald
green Khasi Hills had been a part of Bangladesh. He
had read stories of brutal ethnic cleansing being carried
out in the Chittagong Hill Tracts by the Bangladeshi
Government. A recent Amnesty International report
had cited forced conversions and executions of civilians
including women and children by the Bangladeshi
Rifles. 'Whew'! Lang breathes, 'Maybe, I should not
be too critical of the current situation. Despite the
dysfunctional ministers, the inefficient systems, the
corruption and the scams we still have a functional
government. Here, we do not need to look over our
shoulder and see the shadow of a gun. We have a
Constitution which despite its several flaws protects the
rights and promotes the welfare of its minorities and the
tribes. And Meghalaya is only four decades old and we
are not doing too badly as it is. For once Lang sees some
hope on the horizon and maybe he should not be too
disconsolate with the present state of affairs. But why
did Mills change his mind? Asks Lang. It was becoming
evident that most of his recommendations found their
way to Mountbatten and was passed on to Radcliffe
when he was drawing the border lines. Why were the
Chittagong Hill Tracts obviously swapped with present
Meghalaya? Lang's excitement mounts even further and

he resumes his reading albeit with some difficulty in deciphering some of the passages.

I had intended to turn in my final suggestions today being a Friday but after a final revision of the note discovered that there are some typographical errors. So I will retype the draft and submit it on Monday morning as soon as I reach the office. So far, we are untouched by the chaos and bloodshed which is going on in some parts of the mainland. The Hindu-Muslim massacres in Calcutta have not had any repercussions in this part of the world. Unlike my colleagues posted elsewhere in the country, we still have time to engage in other activities apart from office work. In fact, I am looking forward to my usual round of golf on Sunday at the Shillong Golf Course. Developed in 1898 as a 9-hole golf course by two officers who were members of my service, it was later converted to its present 18 holes in 1924 by Captains Jackson and C.K. Rhodes. Located at an altitude of about 4500 feet above sea level, it still reminds me of the Gleneagles Course in Scotland where I had played several rounds during some of my annual leaves.

The entire course is surrounded by picturesque villages on its eastern side and hills on the other. Some public roads run through some areas of the course and though cars and pedestrians are few, we sometimes need to take care when hitting over them. In fact, just about a month or so ago, a little boy was struck by a ball hit by an army officer. Be that as it may, Mr. H.G. Dennehy, the Chief Secretary of Assam will be my partner in the four ball match against Mr. A.H.S. Fletcher ICS, who was the Deputy Commissioner of the District till the other day and a Brother M.G. McCarthy who it seems was the amateur golf champion of County Cork, Ireland in his younger days. He now teaches physics in St. Edmunds School here in Shillong and plays to a six handicap. My favorite hole is the 6th as it measures about 600 yards in length. Brother Shannon, I was told, reached the green in three shots and almost made a birdie! I must again remind the Club Secretary, though to do something about the dense foliage on the 9th Hole particularly on the right side of the fairway. It seems he is quite distracted by his love affair with Colonel Adler's Khasi wife!

Lang smiles as he reads these lines. And he can imagine the strength and technique of the good Brother McCarthy when you take into account the golf clubs they played with in those days. Hickory shafts were tied onto club heads made of hardwood. Now, you have all types of shafts made of graphite with obscenely oversize club heads. You can buy golf clubs which are designed with deep club faces and undercut cavity system for distance and feel. The balls themselves were primitive and were simply hard rubber balls coated with Brazilian sap and painted over. Now, you could buy multi component balls with radical dimple design and 2G soft compression aided for flight and spin. How the game has changed but the rules and procedures are still almost intact, gratefully thinks Lang. And, yes, despite all these improvements in the technology, skill is still the dominant factor. He reads on . . .

When I was posted to Shillong, in the first few months, I missed my life in the Naga Hills. Though life there was hard at times, this was compensated by the results of my labor. I was able to bring about some changes to the living conditions of the tribes by providing easier access to medical care. Good work in the field of dispensing justice and promoting mutual co-existence between the feuding tribes had lead to a decrease in their headhunting activities. My introduction of the Dobashi system with magistrates selected from their chieftains has also been a remarkable success. However, over the years I have settled down comfortably in this lovely town. Shillong has an excellent club, the Shillong Club which is a walking distance from my residence near the Pinewood Hotel. I hardly need to use my Model T car except for commuting to the Shillong Golf Club and driving to places like Cherrapunji. I often take long walks by the Umkhrah River on the road connecting the Nongmynsong and the Polo Bazar. The waters are azure blue and teeming with brown mahseer and other local fishes. Anglers are aplenty and no one returns home empty handed. The view of the race track and the Polo Ground in the middle is simply superb from across the river and I can even see parts of the 1ˢᵗ Hole lying adjacent to the Club House.

As I have mentioned earlier, the Shillong Golf Course is outstanding and with a length of almost 7000 yards. The Par 4 first hole is a dogleg and lies adjacent to the Polo Grounds with the green located across the road on the left of the clubhouse if you are standing in front of it. The clubhouse itself was constructed in 1925 and it reminds me of the ones we have in England with its high ceilings, slanting roof and elegant bay windows. In 1945, we were witness to an addition made to the rear of the building. Some U.S. Army officers who were posted in the area

***constructed a card room and which has added to the
entertainment facilities offered by the Golf Club.***

Lang can proceed no further as the end portion
of the journal is missing or totally burnt. He is ruing
the fact that he may not be able to find out the reason
as to why Mr. Mills changed his mind regarding the
attachment of present day Meghalaya with the new state
of East Bengal. And why were the Chittagong Hill Tracts
substituted its place? He shakes his head in sadness when
he thinks about the polluted Umkhrah River and the
ugly concrete structures which have come up all along on
the banks of the river. He thinks remorsefully about the
encroachments on the Golf Course, in particular the ones
on the 15th Hole and the disregard the public are having
for the heritage course. But, on the other hand, could the
situation have been worse if had been included in East
Pakistan? Would he have been able to play golf and have
a role in shaping the future of his people? Would there
still be a golf course or would it have been converted into
a mosque or madrassa complex? Lang knows that all of
these questions would be left unanswered.

Lang however has still not given up hope on finding
an answer to Mr. Mills' change of mind and change of
heart. He plans to follow a lead which was suggested by
one of his colleagues, Peter Warren when they met for
their daily lunch on Monday. After narrating about his
experience with the journal and the loss of its end pages,
Warren who was a thoughtful officer had suggested that
newspapers circulated during the time of Partition could
perhaps shed some light on the matter. The following day,
Lang takes time out from his office work after the lunch
break and heads for the nearby State Central Library
located opposite the Church of North India, whose stone

building was completely destroyed in the Great Earthquake of 1897 but was reconstructed in a style similar to that of the Governor's House. Libraries of late are almost deserted due to the information explosion and entertainment found on the Internet, Lang observes. Gone are the days when libraries were always crowded and you have to wait for weeks to borrow the latest Louis L'Amour or an Agatha Christie novel. He appreciates the efforts made by the organizers of the CALM Literary Festival to educate young readers with the simple joy of reading. All those violent video games on the Internet and trashy serials on TV are really affecting the mental capacity of our kids, he feels. He searches for the shelves in which past issues of the Gauhati based paper,' The Assam Tribune' are stored. The paper was started sometime in 1935 and with some luck, he can obtain some information on the events leading up to the Partition of India and the aftermath.

Lang locates old issues of the 'Assam Tribune' but none before the nineteen fifties. He finds out that the permanent Library building was constructed sometime in the middle of 1950 and hence any older records kept elsewhere could have been misplaced or destroyed. He is at a loss and makes his way back to the office. He still does not want to abandon his quest and back in his office, he types in the keywords, 'The Partition of India with reference to East Bengal' in Google Search. He finds quite a bit of information on Wikipedia but of no use to him. One piece of information which pops up constantly is the fact that Cyril Radcliffe destroyed all records relating to the Partition of India. Over lunch on the following day, Peter is disappointed that the lead has fizzled out to the extent that he neglects to partake of the Thai prawn curry cooked by his wife.

-9-

Sitting in his office on Thursday morning while reading the Telegraph newspaper, his mobile phone rings. It is Peter. 'Arvan', he says, 'I found out from my Archivist in the Arts and Culture Department that the district library functioned from the Brahmo Samaj Building near the incomplete Crowborough Hotel in Police Bazar. You could go over and have a look if you like'. Lang thanks him for the tip and plans to visit the library the next day. 'Gosh', he thinks, 'How time flies. It's almost the end of the week and very soon I will be retired and idling around with nothing to do'. Thinking about this, he decides to leave office early and calls for his driver.

The short drive to Police Bazaar takes a long time due to the usual traffic snarls. Enroute, they are slowed down in front of the Deputy Commissioner's office which is housed in a faceless concrete building with narrow aluminum alloy windows. The earlier building had caught fire and burnt down to the ground. It was so impressive, with its wide verandahs, large bay windows and tall timber doors, remembers Lang. Buildings are good indicators of the quality of governance and public service, Lang thinks; secrecy and claustrophobia versus openness and transparency.

The car stops again this time in front of the Shillong Club. This building was devastated by the

1897 Earthquake but rebuilt soon after and did not suffer the fate of the DC's office and his office. It is an impressive building with recessed windows, sloping red roofs and a spacious courtyard. During James Mill's time, it was a whites' only facility and was reputed to be one of the best clubs in the Province of Assam. Lang although a permanent member, seldom visits the club though it has tennis courts and excellent billiard tables. It has, he muses from being a 'Whites Only' to become a 'Gamblers Only' domain which is one of the reasons why he avoids going to the Club. He passes by on the right of the old Assembly compound and where the old imposing Assembly Building used to be located. It burnt down completely due to the negligence of the officer in charge in cleaning the chimneys. Fires and earthquakes have indeed demolished many heritage buildings in the town. His phone rings. "What now? He asks himself. It is Sanbor informing that he will not be playing on the weekend. Lang is sure that his once close friend is spending more time with his mistress, though Sanbor had given the reason that he would be out on tour. He feels sorry for him but he feels sorrier for Daphisha and her two children.

He finally reaches his destination and much to his surprise notices that the compound is now dominated by a hotel called the 'Bram Home'. "Sweet home away from home' proclaims the sign at the entrance. He thinks that it is indeed ironic that the Shillong Chapter of the Brahmo Samaj Movement started by the great reformer Raja Rammohan Roy to fight casteism and materialism has set up a hotel in his memory. A sign of the times, chuckles Lang to himself. He is apprehensive that the little library may have been torn down—another little piece of the town's heritage lost, but to his relief locates the house, still well kept and almost in the same condition when he visited it last in 1978. He recalls that along with his close classmate and friend, Bonnie, he had permanently borrowed a book, 'Shakespearean Tragedy' authored by A.C. Bradley, the famous Shakespearean critic when he was preparing for his BA (English Honors) exam. 'Strange', Lang ruminates, 'school ties really do bind'. Though he meets Bonnie once in two years as he works in Delhi, he feels closer to him than to Sanbor who has been his colleague and friend for almost a quarter of a century.

He enters the musty library and is greeted by a very old Bengali gentleman. 'Can I help you in any way' queries the old man. Lang tells him that he is trying to locate back issues of the Assam Tribune pertaining to the period between April and June of 1947. He is directed to a musty back room full of angled flat shelves on which old newspapers have been arranged. He is impressed to find that the newspapers have been arranged year wise and month wise. He spots old issues of the 'Statesman' and the 'Hindu' but disregards them as he is sure that local news would be featured only in the good old 'Assam Tribune'.

Two hours later, a dusty and visibly tired Lang is about to give up the ghost. He is no closer to finding out what he wants. Though he has considerably enhanced his knowledge about the events and happenings in Shillong and Gauhati during the months leading up to Independence, he has not come across any reference to any report on the circumstances and events leading up to the partition of Assam. He jumps ahead to some June editions and reads about the controversial announcement of Mountbatten on 3ʳᵈ June 1947 regarding the Partition Plan. The power struggle between Nehru and Sardar Vallabhai Patel is a recurring feature. 'Sir', a voice jerks him out of his thoughts. It is the old caretaker who informs that he has to close for the day. Lang takes out another issue of the Assam Tribune and decides that this will be the last one. He has mentally given up and is reconciled to the fact that Mill's secret has gone with him to his grave.

The paper is dated 14ᵗʰ May, 1947 and Lang wearily reads more news items criticizing the British government's inability to send troops to control bloody conflicts between Hindus and Muslims in the province of Punjab. He reads about the deaths caused by floods in Upper Assam. Overall, the news is focused on the impending handing over by the colonial rulers and the plans of the Indian National Congress. But there is no reference to Sir Andrew Clow or his Secretary, Mr. J.P. Mills. 'Damn', utters Lang. 'What the fuck am I doing here. It is almost 6 p.m.?' He sees three missed calls on the touch-screen of his Samsung smart mobile phone and they are all from Rita. He suddenly remembers that he had promised to attend a birthday party of one of her nieces. Now he will be in trouble. She has her own way of getting back; assymetrical warfare, he calls it. No proper breakfast, no nice dinner for the next two weeks. Well, he better get a move on . . .

As he hurriedly gets up, his elbow nudges the newspaper to the ground and he bends down to pick it up. A news item on the second last page—Page 7 catches his eye. It reads as follows:

'LOCAL SHAMAN CURES GOVERNOR'S SECRETARY OF DEADLY SNAKEBITE'.

By Our Reporter

Mr. J.P. Mills ICS, Secretary to the Government of Assam returned to work today after having fully recovered from the ill effects caused after having been bitten by a banded krait, whose venom is considered even more deadly than the king cobra. It was reported that the unfortunate incident occurred on 4th May 1947 at the Shillong Golf Course. Apparently, on the 9th Hole, he marginally sliced his drive and his ball landed in the rough on the right side of the fairway. While he was about to play his second shot, he happened to step on the banded krait. Fortunately, his fellow players, the Chief Secretary, Mr. Fletcher I.C.S. who was till the other day the District Commissioner and one Brother McCarthy were at hand to carry him immediately to the Roberts Hospital.

Though an anti venom serum was administered within an hour of the mishap, Mr. Mills unfortunately slipped into a semi-coma and could not be restored to his full senses even after two days. This reporter was informed by Brother McCarthy that one local healer, a Mr. Banshan Nongbri of Nongjrong Village was summoned in desperation by Dr. Roberts and after the uttering of a few 'mantras' and application of an unknown herbal paste. Nongbri was able to bring about a dramatic improvement in the condition of poor Mr. Mills. (However, it was found out that even after being

discharged; Mr. Mills still had to undergo further treatment for another week at his residence . . .

Lang thanks the old caretaker and directs his driver to take him home. He believes he knows what the main ingredient was in the herbal paste. Must have been the broad green leaves of the rare mongoose plant, he thinks. Small comfort indeed! His investigations have run aground. Somewhere though in the back of his mind there is a lingering thought which he cannot give full expression to. He feels that this is something akin to forgetting a word but which is lying on the tip of one's tongue. Later in middle of the night, tossing around on his bed, an answer suddenly dawns on him. He sits up in bed and . . .

Was it perhaps possible that Mr. Mills underwent a change of heart and mind after being cured by a Khasi healer, Lang thinks? His previously held opinion of our culture and heritage could have been influenced through his interactions with Bah Nongbri and closely understanding traditions, our unique system of governance and our ability to cure serious ailments. Mills ever the inquisitive anthropologist must have surely absorbed and appreciated the sophistication and efficacy of our matrilineal system, our integrated political, social and religious structures. Explaining this later to Peter over lunch, he concludes. "After forming his opinion about the Khasis and why they should be included in East Bengal, Mills apart from his gratitude after being saved from a sure death, must have realized that our tribe with its distinctive identity would have been vaporized in the new dispensation where Muslims formed the majority. We would not have been able to withstand the effects caused by such sudden and extreme change. And *such was his gratitude that he may have inserted a fresh recommendation. And accordingly, could he perhaps have amended those sections in his partition proposal and replaced present day Meghalaya with the Chittagong Hill Tracts before submitting his final recommendations through Sir Clow to Lord Mountbatten'!*

THE END